"You want me to marry Stuart?"

Gerda gasped in astonishment. "You're mad! Stuart's not in love with me and I'm not in love with him. How can you suggest such a cold-blooded arrangement? It's the most heartless—"

"*Heartless* is an ironic accusation from your lips," Jordan said coldly, "and *love* an even emptier protest. What do you know of love? You speak of trust and understanding and unselfishness when the real motive is self-love. Wanting and taking, but pretending it's giving." He tightened his grip on her shoulders, and when she moved her head frantically he laughed softly and raked her throat with his mouth.

Gerda gave a small cry and twisted free. "I loathe you," she choked. "You're the most callous man I've ever known. You—"

"You'd better be thankful, then," he said, "that you're not marrying me."

Harlequin Presents Collection

A new series... of old favorites!

Harlequin has been publishing its widely read *Presents* series for more than eight years. These beautiful romance novels, written by the world's most popular authors of romantic fiction, have become the No. 1 best-selling love stories in more than eighty countries.

Now we are pleased to make available to you, our more recent readers, a chance to enjoy many of the early *Presents* favorites you may have missed.

We know you'll enjoy these carefully selected volumes. They come from our not-too-distant past—a past we are proud of, a past we are sure you'll love!

MARGERY HILTON

a man without mercy

Originally published as Harlequin Presents #52

Harlequin Books

TORONTO • LONDON • LOS ANGELES • AMSTERDAM
SYDNEY • HAMBURG • PARIS • STOCKHOLM • ATHENS • TOKYO

Harlequin Presents edition published July 1974
ISBN 0-373-15008-3

Second printing June 1977
Third printing October 1977
Fourth printing January 1979

This *Harlequin Presents Collection* edition published December 1980

Original hardcover edition published in 1971
by Mills & Boon Limited

CHAPTER I

FRIDAY: another weekend to face.

Gerda's steps slowed on the top three stairs. There was no one to notice her pause or the small weary straightening movement of her shoulders before she inserted her key in the door of number 27. There was never anyone to notice in the quiet, discreetly lit corridors of Grafton Mansions. People lived there, many people, behind the satin-maple doors and muted pastel décor, presumably known by name as well as number to the uniformed porter who nodded gravely each morning and evening to Gerda, but people were residents in Grafton Mansions, not neighbours.

The door closed soundlessly behind her, as though into a cushion of velvet, enclosing her in the loneliness within.

Some day she would enter and that dreadful loneliness would have become the peace of a home waiting to welcome its owner at the end of the day, but that day was yet to come, even after nearly six months. They'd been right, she thought forlornly as she filled the small kettle and began to stow her week's supply of groceries into cupboards and fridge. If she'd heeded all the advice given her after Blaise died she would have found another flat, moved to a strange place, even accepted the invitation Blaise's mother had left open indefinitely. But the thought of Blaise's quiet Devon home, sharing an aged woman's memories, had been unbearable, as had been her reluctance to break up the home Blaise had given her with so much devotion.

Perhaps her well-meaning friends were right; perhaps she was foolish to stay with the constant reminders of Blaise surrounding her instead of making a complete break from the memories of a marriage so pitifully short. Less than two years, and no one but herself and Blaise had known those two years had been borrowed time...

The telephone shrilled and she lowered the heat under the kettle before she went through into the lounge. The caller was Kathryn, as she had known it would be, and she smiled faintly as the older woman's voice came volubly over the line.

'No, please count me out, Kath,' she said when at last she could get a word in. 'Yes, I knew Lyle Kerrick was home for a few days—I met his sister the other day, but I'd planned to catch up on a lot of odd chores this weekend and I'd rather not. It's sweet of you, but I——'

'I know,' came the exasperated response, 'you've been under pressure at the office this week and you're a bit tired. Listen, Gerda; it's high time somebody told you some home-truths. You're twenty-two, not forty-two. And it's six months since Blaise died. When are you going to snap out of it?' A sigh came over the wire. 'Why did you take on this job? You should have gone abroad, gone and stayed with your mother for a few months. Darling, you know I'm not trying to interfere, but somebody has to drag you back into circulation. You don't want to stay a widow for ever, do you?'

Gerda's fingers tightened round the receiver. 'That hasn't anything to do with it, honestly. But I'm not coming for a weekend in which the principal aim is to fix me up with an unattached male. Certainly not Lyle Kerrick.'

'And what's wrong with Lyle?'

'Nothing, except that I haven't the slightest intention of angling for an affair with him—or any other man,' she added grimly.

'Who said anything about an affair?' said Kathryn in hurt tones. 'You know what's the matter with you, don't you? It's time some nice male took you out, wined you and dined you, got you deliciously squiffed, and then made love to you. It's the best cure of all.'

'Maybe, if you know exactly what you're trying to cure.' A haunted look came into Gerda's eyes and she glanced desperately towards the kitchenette door. 'Listen, Kath, I must go—the kettle's screaming. I know you're trying to help and honestly I appreciate it, but can we leave it over this time and maybe . . .'

'All right.' The other woman sighed. 'But we're not going to let you go on like a drop-out. Blaise wouldn't have expected you to live like a nun for the rest of your life; as it was, that last year was no picnic. Poor Blaise! It must have been heartbreaking for you——'

'Yes, Kath—I'll ring you back—I must go—'bye.' Gerda fumbled the receiver down on to the rest and hurried into the kitchenette. Kathryn was a dear and she meant well, but when she started to get maudlin it was unbearable.

Gerda opened a tin of tongue, sliced a couple of tomatoes and buttered a piece of crispbread, then sat down on the stool at the little breakfast bar to stare at the gay yellow-and-orange-patterned surface with unseeing eyes.

She knew that Kathryn was right. She couldn't go on for ever like this, avoiding invitations, losing herself in her work during the day, spending her leisure hours alone with her own pursuits, unwittingly portraying the perfect picture in which they all believed; the young widow tragically robbed of an idyllic marriage.... If only they knew the truth!

And yet she had loved Blaise, and undoubtedly he had loved her. With Blaise she had found a haven at last, where she could close the door on the past. Suddenly her eyes blurred and she shook her head fiercely. *Why did you have to die, Blaise?* she cried with her inward anguish. *Why?*

Wearily she cleared away her half-eaten meal and settled down with the work she had brought home. There were specifications to copy, a summary that would save time on Monday if she got it done now, and Howard's notes on the tender.... Whatever Kathryn's opinion, the pressure of her job as P.A. to Howard Durrel was a rock in her life. There she was needed and didn't have too much time to brood. She had been fortunate that the vacancy was there at the moment she most needed it. Charingfolds weren't too big, too impersonal; Howard was more like a friend than a boss, even though she had never allowed herself to take advantage of past loyalties....

The keys flew under her fingers and at the back of her mind she wondered how he was getting on with the man from Van-Lorn Electronics. Howard was desperately anxious to get that contract, especially in view of the take-over rumours circulating round V.L. and the Wentford Combine. She was taking the last sheet out of the machine when the door chimes tingled softly. Exclaiming aloud, she hurried in response and fell back with surprise at the sight of the burly, grey-faced man outside.

'Howard! I didn't expect to——' She stopped. One glance told her what was the matter. She took his briefcase from him. 'Come in and sit down. I'll get you some hot milk.'

'No—don't bother.'

8

She ignored his faint protest as he sank down near the fire and hurried into the kitchenette. Quickly she heated some milk and took out the bottle of Aludrox which she kept for these occasional emergencies. Howard suffered from what he called the businessman's scourge—ulcers—and from long experience she knew it was useless to counsel an easing up of his pace.

'Thanks,' he murmured when she went back to him, then added inconsequently, 'You're very like your mother, Gerda. Cool and beautiful on the outside but warm and impulsive inside. What would I do without you?'

'Do as the specialist advised—let him rid you of that old faithful, as you call it.'

'I'm getting too old—and too scared.'

'Nonsense. You'd be a new man.'

'I'm not sure I want to be a new man. Gerda,' he set down the glass, 'I'm sorry to land you with this, my dear, but will you help me out?'

'Of course. Do you want me to drive you home? Call the doctor? Or——' She remembered something and leapt up. 'I'd better call Mr Kingsley and cancel your dinner engagement. There's just time to——'

'No,' Howard's gesture checked her, 'that isn't it. Oh, damnation! This would happen at the worst possible time. Gerda, it happened today. I had a call five minutes after you left the office.'

'You mean . . .?'

He nodded, 'It's official. Van-Lorn have sold out to Wentfords.'

She sat down again. 'You think this will affect us adversely?'

'It can't fail to, if we don't get the renewal of that contract.' A spasm of pain contorted Howard's face and his attempt to ride it was distressing to watch. When it passed he brushed his hand across his brow. 'That's why I came. I can't face a night of over-indulgence. Rich food, drinking until the small hours. You know what it's like.'

Gerda knew only too well. She had seen the results the next morning when a grey-faced man came into the office looking like death; the price of surviving in the cut-throat world of commerce. She said, 'You're not fit to. You'll kill yourself, Howard. Let me cancel it before it's too late.'

'I can't. We've got to get that contract. I want you to deputise for me.'

'Me? Tonight! But I——' She glanced at her watch, then at his worried face. 'Howard, I couldn't deputise for *you*.'

'You're going out?'

'No, but you know the prejudice that still hangs on about women....'

'Nonsense. You'll be wonderful. You know those contract details better than I do. You won't even have to haggle. Just smile at him and he'll sign like a lamb.'

Gerda sighed. She had met Kingsley, the hard-mouthed executive from Van-Lorn, once, a few weeks after she had began to work for Howard, and the memory of him didn't quite key in with Howard's optimism. She said doubtfully, 'Yes, you know I'll do anything I can, but don't blame me if he refuses to talk business with a woman.'

'I won't. I'd have sent young Taylor if he'd got back from Manchester in time, but he doesn't get in until after nine, and with the weekend....' Howard let his words hang and his shoulders slumped with relief. 'This is a weight off my mind. Now, will you use my car or take taxis?'

'Taxis—it saves the parking headache.'

10

'The expense account is open to the skies for this occasion. You have your own card—will you use it and I'll square up with you afterwards?'

She nodded.

'I'll give you some ready cash to be on the safe side.' He peeled off some notes. 'Now, I'll just run through a few points....'

When he had done so and commented ruefully that her grasp of the essentials was better than his own, she shook her head. 'I'm flattered at your confidence in me, but I hope I don't let you down. By the way, where do I meet Mr Kingsley, and when?'

'My God! I'm forgetting the most important thing.' Howard groaned aloud. 'It isn't Kingsley tonight. That was part of the call I had. Wentford's new whizz kid himself is coming.'

'Really!' Her brows went up. 'We're honoured. Which one?'

'Jordan Black himself.'

Jordan Black!

Afterwards she knew that only seconds had elapsed while the name echoed into an increasing chain reaction of sound in her head, but it seemed like an age before she was aware of Howard's voice going on:

'—I guessed that might shake you. But I fancy it may turn out a blessing in disguise. He's as noted for his amours as his business acumen, so turn on the feminine charm full strength, won't you? We——'

Howard stopped, sensing that something was wrong. Gerda's oval face had blanched and her eyes had darkened with shock until they were like great storm-washed violets. She turned away.

'I—I can't do it. I'm sorry. I can't. It's——'

'Why ever not?' Sure that she was merely nervous and having second thoughts, he said briskly, 'You'll be the best ambassadress we ever had. And if what I said worries you ... I can't imagine your head being easily turned, even by Jordan Black. You'll just have to put on your man-proof armour. Now stop worrying. You've nothing to worry about.'

Gerda did not hear him. Jordan Black, of all men! The last man in the world she wanted to see again. It was too much to pray that it wasn't him. The universe couldn't hold two Jordan Blacks. Fear turned her skin clammy and her limbs to water. She couldn't do it. Not meet Jordan Black, not after ... not even for Howard, or Charingfolds, or anything. She opened her mouth to cry that she couldn't go through with it, that she'd do anything rather than ... then she saw Howard's pain-lined features, the anxiety in his eyes, and she remembered the other pieces out of the past that made up life's jigsaw. Twenty years ago Howard Durrel had seen her father through that crisis. Ten years ago he had been a rock when her father died, and six months ago he had been her salvation when she lost Blaise. If a quirk of fate hadn't taken him out of the country four years ago the greatest crisis she had ever faced wouldn't have happened, with the repercussions that at this very moment were threatening the frail foundations on which she had painfully rebuilt her life. With an effort she assumed an icy calm and forced the fear back. She couldn't fail Howard, whatever the cost.

'I'm sorry,' she said shakily, 'just nerves. Where do I meet him?'

'I'm not with it, my dear,' he exclaimed ruefully. 'Eighty-thirty, at Toby's. A man's haunt, I'm afraid. I'd forgotten that angle.'

'I don't mind for once.'

'He does the best steak in town, but for you ... the Savoy Grill or the Looking Glass would have been a more suitable setting. Perhaps Black might care to go somewhere else.' Howard's voice faded again and his mouth went taut.

'It doesn't matter. I'd better get changed.'

'Yes.' Howard got slowly to his feet. 'Will you know Black?'

Will I know Jordan Black! She nodded. 'Don't worry, I won't miss him. And you go straight to bed and call the doctor, do you hear?'

'Yes. Here's the contract. He won't sign it—tonight's just a warm-up, but you'd better have it. Thanks a lot, my dear. If you're not too late back you could ring me, if not ...'

'Tomorrow.'

When he had gone a dreadful silence closed in on her. She showered and sorted fervently through her wardrobe for something suitable for the occasion. The nylon jersey classic was too white and sophisticated for Toby's, the lurex was out, the jade shift was a trifle *outré*, the blue too filmy ... it would have to be the rose Banlon ... hair up with this ... no jewellery ... not too much make-up...

Her fingers were like ice when they touched perfume to wrists and throat, and her reflection stared back from the mirror, mocking her haunted eyes, the pale perfect oval under the severely swathed spun-gold hair. Jordan Black had probably forgotten her existence, probably wouldn't even recognise her. It was three years ago. She was no longer the nineteen-year-old with shoulder-length tresses flowing free, with the soft roundness of immaturity still lingering where now the fine bone structure showed clear and pure at cheek and jawline.

Gerda took a deep breath and donned her wrap. What could Jordan Black do to her now? It was all in the past. No man could hold animosity dear all these years. Surely he didn't still hate...

* * *

He was the first man she saw as she walked into Toby's.

All the way across town she had despised herself for the hope that something had delayed him, that he might be prevented from keeping the appointment, and by the time she paid off the taxi-man she had almost convinced herself that it was going to be that way. Until she walked into the warm smokiness and the masculine heaviness of mahogany panelling, Regency flocked wall covering of maroon and ivory, the guns and eighteenth-century sporting prints above buttoned leather banquettes, and saw Jordan Black lounging at the far end of the bar, a half tumbler of whisky in one negligent hand and a cigarette smouldering in the fingers tapping restlessly on the bar corner.

She stood within the shadows of the entrance, unheeding of the male heads turning towards her, the only woman to invade their sanctum. But Jordan Black had not yet seen her and the overwhelming impulse came to run.

He hadn't changed one iota.

The thick silver hair still ruffled carelessly above the deep forehead and the heavy brows that were so startlingly dark in contrast. The wide square chin with the cleft in it was as jutting and pugnacious as ever, the mouth still parted with that curiously careless thrust of the lower lip and spoke of an innate sensuousness, and all the six-foot length of him conveyed the power and arrogance of a man to whom black was black and white was white and all the indeterminate inbetween simply didn't exist.

Still he didn't look up. It wasn't too late.

Gerda took a step forward and donned a cloak of desperate defence. She spoke to the barman, he nodded, gestured, and she walked firmly towards the man at the end.

'Good evening. Mr Black?'

He turned his head lazily, the dark blue eyes under their black lashes cool in their regard. His head inclined slightly.

She forced her 'client' smile, charming, impersonal, yet with warmth. 'I'm sorry to tell you that Mr Durrel is indisposed. It was too sudden to leave time to cancel the appointment.'

He continued to look hard at her, not helping her.

'We didn't want to cause you inconvenience. Mr Durrel asked me to come along in his place.' She made a small gesture to the folder she carried. 'I have all the details here, if you'd care to discuss them ... I think I can clear up any points you might want clarified.'

'The new contract for Charingfolds?'

'Yes.' Her lips felt taut and dry under the pale rose colour that echoed her dress. 'Would you care for another drink, Mr Black, or would you prefer to eat straight away?'

'I dislike being entertained by a woman.' He looked over her head and the barman came instantly. 'What will you have, Miss——?' He paused deliberately on the title.

'Mrs Manston,' she said clearly, with equal emphasis. 'A Bronx, thank you.'

'Cigarette?' The case flipped open, plain on one side, tipped at the other. The lighter appeared, snapped on, with that smooth sleight of hand you hardly saw. It flicked into flame a second time. 'You're not lit.'

The tremor of her fingers was more pronounced this time. She picked up her drink and inwardly she was seething. This was worse than all her worst imaginings.

She said, 'If you'd prefer to postpone the discussion until Mr Durrel is better . . .'

'I don't. What's the matter with him?'

'Ulcers. And he refuses to take time off for treatment.'

Jordan Black shrugged. 'He won't, if he's worried about competitors waiting to cut his throat. For how long have you supplied Van-Lorn?'

'Five years.'

'And you have the capacity to supply us?'

A fraction of the tension eased out of her. She could answer these questions promptly and lucidly, and the technicalities did not cause her to stumble.

He pushed his glass away. 'Let's eat.'

Silently she moved with him, aware of the subtle change of roles as the waiter deferred automatically to him and that she was moving on shifting sand. Howard had made the biggest misjudgement of his life when he confidently asserted that she could play the role of business host. With any normal charming man she might have succeeded, but Jordan Black was not a normal charming man. He was so male he intimidated, and the idea of a woman executive entertaining him was doomed to failure from the start.

He chose the wine, ordered her grapefruit cocktail and a prawn cocktail for himself and the steaks to follow, then he put his elbows on the table and leaned forward.

'Now tell me why you're here.'

She started. 'I've told you why. You must have been aware of this contract under discussion or you

16

wouldn't have been here tonight.'

'What exactly is your position in the firm?'

'P.A. to Mr Durrel.' She dipped carefully into the grapefruit.

'I see. Is he the only director in the firm?'

Her mouth tightened. Hadn't he seen any of the correspondence? Acquainted himself no matter how briefly with the matter before he set off? If not, why hadn't he let Kingsley carry on the negotiations? Well, if he wanted the firm's history...

'Mr Merrick's on leave. Mr Taylor is in Manchester on business. There was a strike at——'

'I know all about the stoppages at Dellows,' he interrupted. 'I'm not concerned with the unnecessary details at the moment'

'What is it you want to know, Mr Black?' she said quietly.

'Is this the way you do business, Gerda?'

The moment had come. His eyes were cold, compelling her to hold their stare. Her mouth went dry and the background noises of the dining room merged into a curious rushing sound. She said in a choked voice: 'Why didn't you say that before?'

'Why didn't *you* choose to recognise me?'

She could find no words of defence, and he said: 'You don't change. Only you would have the nerve to come here. But of course,' his mouth curled down, 'being the only woman in this dining room is child's play to your exhibitionistic little ego.'

She recoiled as though he had struck her. Wildly she groped for her bag. 'If that's the case I'd better leave.'

'And make a scene? Stay where you are! What about the contract?'

She glimpsed a waiter hovering by the alcove and subsided. 'You don't change, Jordan. And you don't forget.'

'Did you expect me to?'

'No, I'd be a fool if I expected anything from you,' she said bitterly. 'Least of all, understanding.'

She bent her head, seizing at the pretence of eating and knowing food would choke her. She saw the light reflect on his wine glass, the flash repeated as he set it down.

He said, 'So Blaise died six months ago. Are you still a widow? Or is Howard Durrel the new candidate?'

With quiet deliberation she pushed her plate away and sat up very straight. 'You know very well that you have the advantage at present. If you must insult me I've no option but to allow you that satisfaction,' she said evenly. 'But out of a respect for a man who is completely blameless, and who had nothing whatsoever to do with anything concerning you and me, I must ask you to leave Howard Durrel out of it.'

'It seems you're learning loyalty,' he commented dryly. 'It's a pity you didn't acquire it a bit earlier.'

'I'm not going to argue,' she said coldly. 'I came here to discuss business, not to—not——' her voice wavered and with an effort she regained control—'not to start the old useless recriminations all over again. Now, may we return to the purpose of this meeting?'

'Ah, yes. The contract.' Jordan leaned back and surveyed her with cynical eyes. 'You want this contract very badly, don't you? Charingfolds had a bad year last year.'

'It comes to all firms at some time.' She kept her face expressionless, knowing he was finding a sadistic satisfaction in tormenting her. 'Aren't you going to have dessert?'

He gave a gesture of negation and asked for the cheese-board. When the waiter had gone Jordan said slowly: 'Very well—business. I presume you're in Durrel's confidence ... there is a great deal I want to know before I commit myself.'

It was a dreadful meal. As though he shrugged into another garment Jordan Black became the hard inhuman man of commerce he was reputed to be. The quesions he fired at her became an inquisition; every point in the contract was analysed and fought over, and Gerda felt her nerves straining to snapping point long before he finally stopped and lit yet another cigarette.

The dining room had almost emptied and the air was heavy with cigar fumes. She watched Jordan tug at his lower lip and she remembered Howard saying: '*He won't sign tonight, you know. This is only a preliminary warm-up,*' and the chill of despair stole over her. She did not believe that he had the remotest intention of awarding the contract to Charingfolds—not now, not now he'd found she was involved.

She stayed silent, the enquiry in her eyes patent enough, and he said suddenly: 'Let's get out of here.'

That brought another uncomfortable impasse. Totally ignoring her protests, he produced an American Express card, settled up everything, and told the tired-looking barman to 'have one on me', as he escorted her out.

'I never allow women to entertain me—financially, that is,' he said brusquely when they emerged into the darkness. 'Well,' he faced her, 'where do we go from here?'

She stared and he gave a short laugh. 'Nothing's cut and dried yet, you know. For one thing, that guarantee clause on delivery schedules isn't watertight enough for me. Come on, my car's just round the corner. We'd better go back to my place.'

'No!'

The exclamation escaped too quickly and he said sharply: 'Why not? It's where I usually wind up these sessions.'

'I'd rather not. It's—it's getting very late, and——' She stopped uneasily.

'And you're afraid of your reputation,' he said scornfully. 'Sure that's all?'

'That's all.'

'You believe it yourself! No, you don't change one bit, Gerda. That cool, innocent beauty. Calculated to fool any man. But it doesn't fool me.'

'I think I'd better go.' She looked at a point just beyond his shoulder. 'I'll pass on your comments to Mr Durrel and ask him about the guarantee clause. He'll get in touch with you as soon as possible.' She held out her hand. 'Goodnight, and thank you for the meal.'

He ignored her hand. 'Where are you going?'

'Home, of course.'

'By car?'

'A taxi.'

'I'll drive you home.'

'No.' She backed a pace. 'There's no need to bother. I can get a taxi quite easily.'

'Maybe. I don't leave women alone in the street at one o'clock in the morning.' He took her arm and propelled her across the road. Her reluctance was not lost on him as they approached the sleek opulent lines of the green Mercedes. He said grimly as he unlocked the door: 'Don't worry. I know what you're thinking. But I'd have to be screaming for a woman before I'd touch *you!*'

He seized the folder from her and threw it into the back of the car. 'Where to?' he said to the stiffly averted profile.

She made no move to enter the car. 'It must give you a great satisfaction to hate me like this.'

'No. Not hate.' He held open the door and put a hand on her shoulder. 'Hatred is too akin to love, my dear Gerda. And I doubt if you know the full meaning of either emotion. If you had ...' he drew her back against him, 'I doubt if you'd have been here tonight.'

She shivered under his hands and abruptly ducked into the car. Every instinct urged her to storm at him, to beg him to try to understand, to escape before control finally snapped. But she could do none of these things that instinct urged, only huddle back against the soft smooth leather and pray for strength to withstand his torment until she had completed her mission. After that ...

The vehicle vibrated as Jordan Black swung in behind the wheel and slammed the door. His arm brushed hers as he flicked at switches and she flinched. To be enclosed in the darkness of the car with him was almost unbearable, and she started when he spoke, the sharpened perception of her fear making her seek the menace in his tone.

But he merely said flatly: 'Where did you say?'

'Grafton Mansions.'

'I know it.' The car eased forward, responsive to every touch; obedient, unresisting as a woman might be under his hands, was the thought that flashed into her mind. As she had been that night three years ago. Did he remember? Was he thinking of that last time she had been in a car with him? After they'd left the hospital and she'd tried to tell him the truth about herself and Stuart? When she'd tried to explain, to defend herself? She'd wept, because it was so tragic and there was nothing she could do, and he'd taken her in his arms. She'd believed she had his understanding, that he would comfort her, and the comfort had become his kisses, embraces that drew unbelievable wonder from her. Instantly she had believed that he cared about her after all and because of that exquisite belief she'd forgotten everything and cradled that silvery head in her hands, surrendering with joyous abandon to the passion she believed was his love.

Gerda closed her eyes. The scar was as agonising as though it were only yesterday when it had been inflicted. She could still feel the aching pressure of his hands, hear his scornful laugh as he thrust her away from him, the cruel, unforgivable accusations he had hurled at her. That she was cheap, worthless, and selfish, and that till the end of his days he'd never forgive her for the tragedy she had brought on his brother.

When the car stopped and he turned to her she braced herself for his anger, the two levels of time still confused in her brain, and she saw his smile.

'I'm afraid we'll have to continue the session later. When will you see Durrel?'

'Tomorrow morning. It's too late tonight to phone him.'

She took the folder, looked at him uneasily, not trusting that smile. 'I'll get in touch with you first thing Monday morning.'

'That's too late. I'll be in Paris.'

'For how long?'

'A day. Then Bonn. I should be back in town by Thursday.'

She regarded him steadily. 'It'll have to be Thursday.'

He rested one arm along the back of the seat and considered her from under those dark brows. 'You're letting me slip away very easily. You're not cut out for this job, you know.'

'Really?' Her mouth compressed.

'A man would have pinned me down long before this—metaphorically speaking, of course.'

'Of course.' She knew he was still playing with her. 'And a gentleman's handshake on it.'

His smile flickered. 'You still believe commerce is a gentlemanly business?'

'In Charingfold's—yes.' She tucked the folder under her arm and once again offered her hand. 'Goodnight. Thank you for the lift.'

He did not move. 'Haven't you forgotten something?'

'I don't think so.'

'Aren't you going to ask after Stuart?'

The colour fled from her face. 'Will it make it any better if I do?' she said in a low voice. 'How is he?'

'Resigned to being a cripple for the rest of his life. They didn't hold out much hope, *if* you remember.'

'I do remember—I'm not likely to forget.'

'No? I find your forgetfulness more convincing than your memory.'

'You've made that perfectly convincing—right from the start.' She fumbled for the door catch and thrust her way out on to the forecourt. 'What do you expect me to do now? Say I'm sorry for something I'm not guilty of? Send my polite regards? What good will it do now?'

'None at all.' His eyes glittered like black ice and he leaned over to pull the door shut. 'Because you never cared.'

The crack of the door split the night's silence and the engine surged into power. The braking lights blinked on like angry eyes as the car slowed at the drive-out, then disappeared across the intersection. Silence settled again.

Gerda found herself in the lift without consciously remembering getting there, and the sickening little sensation closed round the pit of her stomach as it stopped at the second floor and the doors slid open soundlessly. The weakness of reaction spread through her limbs and when she entered the flat she was forced to sink down in a chair before even taking off her jacket.

The soft creamy fur slid from her shoulders unheeded while she regained sufficient control to get up and pour herself a drink. Although the flat was warm enough she felt numbed, all except the feverish action of her brain. As though recorded on a mental monitor screen, the evening rolled back relentlessly; Jordan Black standing at the bar, facing her across a table, his eyes accusing her. . . . Surely after three years his power to tear her apart should have waned: but it hadn't. . . .

Staring into the shadows that night she tried to seize at reassurance, at the knowledge that Howard would have recovered by Thursday. There was no reason why she should have to see Jordan Black again. Once again the past could sink into oblivion.

But there was no peace in the thought. With the certainty of the ordained she knew the futility of the hope; Jordan Black had not done with her yet.

CHAPTER II

FOREBODING still lay like a weight on Gerda when she wakened to the grey wet light of Saturday's dawn. The sleepless hours had painted their own blue brushmarks under her eyes and dimmed the delicate rose and cream of her colouring.

She picked at her breakfast, eked out the time until she could phone Howard, and when the hands touched nine she threw down the morning paper and hurried to the phone.

The ringing tone remained unanswered, and reluctantly she replaced the receiver. If he'd had a bad night he might have slept late and Mrs Sanders, his housekeeper, had probably gone out shopping. Gerda stooged restlessly round the flat, torn between the urgency to contact Howard as soon as possible and a wish to consider a sick man's state of mind. Yet if she didn't ring him he might be anxious. She waited until half-past, then made for the phone. As she reached out her hand the bell shrilled with unnerving urgency. Relief chased the minor shock; it would be Howard himself...

She almost spoke his name straight away, then the tumbling, agitated spate of words came through and her eyes widened with shock. 'Oh no!' she murmured. 'No.'

A little while later she put down the phone and gave way to distress. Howard had collapsed late the previous night. His ulcer had perforated and he had been rushed to hospital. He was very ill, Mrs Sanders said.

Gerda pulled herself together. She had forgotten Jordan Black and her own worries in a flood of regret. All last night while she was worrying about herself Howard had been more dreadfully ill than she had suspected. Although Mrs Sanders had telephoned the hospital for news immediately before ringing Gerda, her desire to be told first-hand overruled the normal common sense that said there couldn't possibly be any more news.

The calm tones of the ward sister seemed infuriatingly unhurried. Trying to be calm herself, Gerda explained who she was, and remembering that most hospitals had rules regarding the giving of information about patients only to next of kin she said anxiously: 'Mr Durrel has no close relatives. Apart from a widowed sister-in-law in Scotland he has no one.'

'I see,' said the calm voice, 'in that case . . . Mr Durrel was too ill last night to tell us much and his housekeeper was very upset.'

'How is he?'

'He's still ill, Mrs Manston, but he's comfortable.'

'Can I see him, please?' she begged.

'Just one moment . . .'

There was a long pause, voices in the background, a clatter as though something banged against something, then the sister's voice again. 'Yes, you may visit him this afternoon. Two till four. But will you ask for me before you go in.'

It was a command, not a request, and Gerda assented thankfully. The fact that visiting hours had been mentioned was slightly heartening. She had recollections of her mother's illness four years previously when she had been permitted to visit at any time. They mustn't consider Howard to be dangerously ill. . . .

She began to despair of lunchtime ever coming that day, but at last it did and after it she was able to change and get ready to go to the hospital. Should she take him anything? It was improbable that any food-stuffs would be allowed at this stage, and he'd be too ill to be bothered to read. Had Mrs Sanders remembered all the personal items, a change of pyjamas, toiletries, shaving kit ...? But that could come later. The main thing was to see him.

Even though she was braced to meet illness there was still a sense of shock when she entered the side ward where Howard lay. The big genial man had aged pitifully in the space of a few hours and his face held little more colour than the pillow against which it was framed. There was the daunting array of drip and plasma stands near the bedhead and that tight-tucked, wrinkleless spread of sterile white bedcoverings which seemed to rob the patient of all individuality.

He opened his eyes and recognition glimmered in their weary depths. He tried to smile at her and with a little exclamation she bent impulsively and kissed his cheek.

'Don't try to talk if you don't feel up to it,' she whispered.

'It's good to see you, Gerda.' He made a weak grop-ing movement and she touched his hand, feeling the tears sting at her eyes as she noticed how white and blue-veined it was, betraying the amount of blood he had lost.

She straightened, looking for somewhere to put the big sheaf of flowers—a selection of all the sunshine yellow blooms the florist could offer—she had brought.

He said, 'They're beautiful—you shouldn't have bothered,' as she put them in the hand-basin. When she turned back she saw the questions in his eyes and knew what he wanted to ask.

She sat down by his side. 'I've been warned not to stay too long—and not to worry you. So,' she smiled, 'don't you worry. Just get better.'

'I must know, Gerda, or I will worry. How did it go last night?'

'Fair.' She tried to keep her voice light, knowing she had to be honest. 'He—Jordan Black—didn't commit himself to the point of signing. Exactly as you said. He's going to Paris on Monday, then Bonn, so it'll have to wait until he gets back.'

Howard reflected on this for a moment or so. 'Did he seem favourably disposed?'

'I'm not sure,' she said carefully. 'He seemed inclined not to take me as seriously as I'd have wished.'

'What did I tell you? You charmed him.'

She looked away. 'He insisted on standing the exes.'

Howard gave a faint smile. 'I trust you did remember to mention the contract on the way home.'

'Yes, and several times before that.' Gerda turned as the door opened and the nurse beckoned. 'I'm going to be thrown out. Is there anything I can bring you tomorrow?'

'No, my dear, and there's no need to give up your Sunday to visit me.'

But she knew she would, despite his protest, and by the next afternoon there was a small but marked improvement in his condition. To her relief he did not return to the matter of the contract and she thought thankfully of the respite caused by Jordan Black's trip to the Continent. However, on the Tuesday evening the nurse stopped her as she was about to go into the ward. Conscious of a quiver of unease, she followed the nurse into the office and a moment or so later an elderly doctor entered.

Without preamble he said: 'You're Mr Durrel's

secretary?' When she nodded he waved her to a chair. 'We appreciate that you're anxious to visit him, Mrs Manston, but we're not too happy about certain aspects.'

She stiffened slightly. 'In what way, Doctor?'

'We've had cases like this before. Businessmen, and their visitors bringing their office worries with them. Only last month we had to put a stop to one instance when our patient was literally running his business from his bed. Oh yes, when the paperwork arrived and a tape-recorder we had to call a halt. No,' he held up a hand, 'we're not accusing you of that—yet—just giving you a friendly warning. Something's worrying him, isn't it?'

'Yes, a contract.'

'Well, you've got to allay that worry. It was a near thing with your boss. It could have been his last contract. He lost about forty per cent of his blood, Mrs Manston, and he's not a young man. Have I made myself clear?'

'Perfectly.' She stood up. 'You can trust me. He won't have cause to worry. I'll see to that.'

But could she? She could hush Howard's questions, assure him everything was in hand, promise him she would keep him informed of all developments, but how could she give him the one thing essential to his peace of mind? As the week wore on she grew more worried, knowing the unspoken obsession in Howard Durrel's mind, and by the Thursday she was tense with resolve: somehow she had to get that contract signed. But how?

In theory it seemed straightforward enough. Simply to ask Mr Merrick to cancel everything to chase the Wentford deal and hand the whole thing over to him. But in practice it wasn't quite so simple. Mr Merrick had had to curtail his holiday and return to take over most of Howard's work, and unfortunately, while he was a wizard on the financial side he was not the most diplomatic of men. It had always been Howard who had wined and wooed the clients.

'Very well,' Mr Merrick said unwillingly, when she had made explanations which didn't sound convincing because perforce they concealed the truth, 'if you don't feel you can nail Black. Get him for me.'

'Yes, Mr Merrick,' she said humbly.

But Jordan Black was not available on the three occasions she tried to 'get' him, nor was he available on the Friday.

'Stonewalling,' Mr Merrick grunted. 'Never mind. I might see old Kingsley at the club tonight.'

In her heart she was certain it was a forlorn hope. There was no sentiment in the world of business and she had a suspicion that Kingsley's word would carry little influence now. With Van-Lorn he had wielded considerable power; with Wentfords he was probably wondering at this very moment where *he* was going to wind up.

'If Kingsley hasn't fallen under the axe,' Mr Merrick said dourly, echoing her own thoughts as she put the cover on her machine prior to packing up for the night.

'Will you let me know if you do?' she asked.

'Sure.' A flash of understanding showed in his usually hard face. 'If it's hopeful we tell Howard, if it isn't we don't, eh?'

'Something like that,' she nodded sadly.

He promised to telephone her at the flat the following morning, but up till eleven he had not kept the promise and she concluded he'd failed or forgotten to contact Kingsley. She paced to the window and stared down at the sluggish stream of Saturday morning traffic. The fear wouldn't stay subdued any longer. A star of ill-omen had been shining last weekend. If Howard hadn't taken ill and Jordan Black hadn't set eyes on herself the contract would have been in the bag. Nothing would shake her conviction that it was because of her that he had decided to stonewall all the week. What a fool she'd been to let him realise that his decision could hurt her personally. If only . . .

The green car down below was slowing. There was a snarl-up. A red delivery van badly parked and some-body trying to overtake where they shouldn't. Some drivers were fools. . . . The green car was a Mercedes, it . . . Gerda's detachment fled and she leaned forward till her head bumped against the glass.

The Mercedes slid neatly across the forecourt and the driver got out. The bright sunlight glinted on the ruffled silver hair and flashed blindingly on the door as it slammed shut. Jordan Black glanced up briefly at the façade of high windows and concrete and walked towards the entrance.

That loose-limbed deceptively unhurried gait that was so individual and unmistakable . . . he couldn't be coming *here*!

Gerda stood panic-stricken, then rushed to the mir-ror, stared at the mouth innocent of make-up, and tried to remember something that was missing. No, she wasn't going to fly for comb and lipstick. She wasn't going to answer the door. . . .

When the chimes rang like an amplified carillon and she drew the door open she remembered the absurd omission. She saw the deep blue gaze leave her face and travel down to her stockinged feet and instantly experienced the subtle shift of balance in his favour.

He said, 'Well, are you going to keep me on the doorstep?'

She stood back, trying to equate dignity with shoe-lessness and the loss of a couple of inches she couldn't afford, and gestured towards the lounge door, murmuring an excuse before she darted into the bedroom for shoes.

'With or without—it's the same to me,' he said from the doorway, watching her hurried fumbling into bronze patent sling-backs. 'Actually, the informal image is improved without them.'

'Is it?' She shouldered past him. 'Can I offer you a drink?'

'No. I manage to stay off it till noon.' He followed her into the lounge and dropped lazily into the centre of the studio couch. 'Try me with coffee.'

She could feel his gaze burning into her back as she walked into the kitchenette. Through the divider she saw him light a cigarette and get up to search round for an ashtray, and through his eyes she saw the light spacious room she and Blaise had dressed with silver birch and clear bright blues and greens in the Scandinavian style. He was examining the sepia pastel sketch Blaise had done of her the week after their marriage when she went through with the tray.

He turned. 'As Blaise saw you?'

'One would assume so. Sugar?'

'No, thank you. Husbands should never paint their wives.' He returned to the couch. 'For that matter no man should ever attempt to paint the woman he loves.'

She stayed silent, sitting very straight in the fireside chair.

'The portrait is never true.'

'Is any depiction in two dimensions?'

He shrugged and looked back at the sketch. 'It's an interesting contrast to the camera's eye. Or perhaps you don't agree?'

She stiffened, and he smiled cynically. 'I see you haven't forgotten. Was that why Blaise superimposed his own new impression of Internationale's calendar girl?'

Gerda set her cup down sharply. 'You didn't come here to talk about that. I think you'd better tell me why you *did* come.'

His brows arched. 'An odd question from a girl who has telephoned my office seven times over the past two days.'

'Mr Merrick phoned seven times.'

'Don't quibble. How's Durrel?'

'Slightly improved, but he's still very ill.'

'Any sign of him getting home?'

'Not yet.' She got up to take his empty cup. But the reminder of something she thought long since forgotten had left her unsteady. The cup tipped as she took the saucer from Jordan's hand and the little silver apostle spoon fell to the carpet. Jordan's reflexes were far quicker than her own. He picked it up and took the cup and saucer firmly from her hand.

'You're very jumpy today. Got any engagements this weekend?'

'Why?' She was remembering his abrupt way of switching subjects. 'Did you want to see Mr Merrick?'

'No. If you've got any you'd better cancel them.'

'Just like that?'

He sat down again. 'You've got a busy weekend in front of you.'

'Listen,' she took a deep breath, 'will you tell me straight? What about the weekend?'

'You want to negotiate this contract. Very well; we'll negotiate this weekend. I'm taking you down to Green Rigg. Immediately.'

'But . . .' a rush of panic chased shock, 'I can't. Not at

33

such short notice. And I—I'm going to see Howard tomorrow afternoon. And——'

'He won't mind. It's in his interest. Or is it?'

She hardly noticed the dry implication in the after-question. Go to Green Rigg for the weekend. With Jordan Black. Now. Every sense screamed within her to refuse. This contract wasn't important enough to Wentfords to rate Jordan Black devoting an entire weekend to discussion of it. This was something else, something devious, and it concerned herself. She became aware of him watching her, his expression unmoving and utterly assured. He knew she would fall in with his plans.

She opened her mouth to refuse, then remembered Howard Durrel and knew that this was the end of his hopes to re-coup Charingfolds. It was hopeless; she couldn't fail him now.

'I'll have to pack a few things,' she said, turning away.

'Sure.' He relaxed back and put his feet on the black velvet pouffe. 'Remember it's informal. I can talk business as well on the beach as in the boardroom.'

She could well credit this, but there would be no business on the beach if she could help it, she thought grimly, stowing a crisp white sun-slip into her case as a sole concession towards the bright warm promise the weather held.

The sun brought out the weekend motorists and the influx of traffic on the roads south to the coast kept Jordan Black preoccupied, for which fact Gerda was grateful. It was three years since she had travelled the route down to the small sylvan glen nestling between downs and sea where Jordan's country retreat lay. The route held too many landmarks and made the memories more poignant the nearer they came to their

34

destination. For the moment, being near him was as much as she could take; she needed more time to forge the shield that three years should have rendered unnecessary.

It was nearing four when he swung off on to one of the narrow winding lanes and took the long way round to the village. She forbore to question him when he stopped the car outside a small cottage and said briefly: 'We'll get tea here.'

The tiny parlour held only four tables. Apart from a young couple with a bright-eyed toddler who were preparing to depart, the holidaymakers seemed to have missed this haven for the thirsty. When the tea and buttered scones were brought Jordan took only a cup of tea. 'I said we'd arrive about seven.'

His glance seemed to challenge her to question that, and she shrugged. 'You've got three hours in hand, then.'

'I want to unwind.'

She glanced through the lattice windows and reflected that the peaceful setting seemed an uncharacteristic one in which Jordan Black might unwind. But she restrained any comment, determined not to allow him to disturb her to the point of losing a calm outward mien. Despite this resolve his steady regard was becoming more unnerving every moment and she was thankful when he betrayed a restlessness and they went back to the car.

'Where are we going now?' she asked.

'Just driving around,' he said laconically, and put the car into gear. 'Then we'll walk a bit,' he added. 'I could do with some sea air in my lungs.'

His remarks seemed innocuous enough, but Gerda could not help glancing sideways at him, and then wished she hadn't. He had turned his head, and he inclined it slightly with that mocking little tilt of recognition that also challenged. She tried not to look at the sensuous curve of his lower lip and shook her head as he murmured: 'Any objections?'

Some three or four miles farther on the sea came in sight and the dip that led down to the cove. Jordan stopped the car in a rough naturally formed lay-by clear of the lane and switched off the engine. He turned to her, and Gerda's heart began to bump.

'Well,' he said, 'why don't you come out with it?'

'Come out with what?' Her fingers tightened on the handbag on her lap.

'Why I brought you back here?'

'You wanted some sea air in your lungs.'

'How true!' His mouth curled down at the corners. 'You *don't* change.' He got out and came round to her side, and it was impossible to avoid the hand he put out as she stepped on to the uneven ground.

He retained his grasp on her hand as they began to walk down the rough slope to the beach, and she was certain he knew that she longed to break free and dared not risk the outcome. He began to whistle, softly and tunefully under his breath, as though he did not notice her steps beginning to drag as they neared the hollow under the chalk spur.

He said, apparently casually, 'Are you still a bad sailor?'

'Yes.' The admission was forced from her and she knew what was coming.

'Stuart gave up the boat eventually, you know.'

'He—he would have to. It's a pity. He—he loved sailing.' She licked dry lips and her eyes were tortured as Jordan scrambled up into the hollow and spread out the jerkin he had carried over his arm. He bent over and held out both hands. 'Up you come.'

36

Feeling as though she was being caught tighter and tighter in the web of his power, she grasped his hands and let him pull her up beside him. For a wild breathless moment she thought he was going to keep drawing her on, into his arms, but he released her and gestured mockingly for her to sit down.

'We used to take him aboard, had a special ramp made and adaptions to accommodate his wheelchair, but he hated it. Not being able to take part frustrated him to the point of fury. The trips became a misery for everyone, so at the finish we decided to sell the *Sweet Fay*.'

Jordan dropped down into a relaxed sprawl and stared at the sea. 'After that we gave up trying to get him interested in outdoor pursuits. He refused to learn to drive a special car for the disabled patients, as he refused to countenance *any* form of therapy. He would sit and stare at a book, never turning a page, just brooding. It got so that no one dared say a word. He'd flare into rages. Curse his useless legs. Curse us because we could walk and he couldn't.'

His voice had remained unvarying in its tone, and his profile unmoving. He went on: 'It was like that for months, until my mother had a breakdown. I sent her to Italy, then the Greek islands, with a companion, and I took three months' leave to devote myself to Stuart's rehabilitation. For a while I thought I'd succeeded. Despite himself he found an interest in painting—the ghastly neo-impressionist stuff or whatever they call it. Stuart's paintings were like nightmares, but the main thing was that he was showing interest in something. But I couldn't stay around indefinitely, surrounding him with people and amusements. When he came home I had to settle him down at Green Rigg and he gradually lapsed back into his moods and depression again, but with a slight difference; he accepted his fate.' Jordan moved, and looked straight into Gerda's eyes. 'But he's never forgotten.'

'And neither have you!' Her control snapped. The unchanging, even timbre of Jordan's voice had brought her nerves to unbearable tautness. She raised trembling hands to her face. 'Why?' she choked. 'Why do you go on blaming me for Stuart's being crippled? It was an accident!'

'We know it was an accident. We know Stuart crashed. And I know what made him crash—even though in the end he wouldn't have you blamed.'

'Then why do you persist in blaming me?' she said bitterly.

'Because if you had redeemed your promise it might have been different. But you didn't. You were too damned selfish. A cripple wasn't much use to you, was he?'

She flinched from his scorn and shook her head despairingly. It was hopeless to convince Jordan of the harshness of his judgement. Three years ago she had tried; then, as now, he had chosen to believe the worst of her. She said dully, 'That's why you brought me here, isn't it? To open it all up again. To work off your hatred and bitterness. Stuart never hated me like that, and he was hurt most of all. But all you're obsessed with is your desire for revenge. But why? What have I ever done to you? And what good can it do now?' she ended bitterly.

He shrugged, seeming unmoved by her distress. 'I don't know. I only know that when you walked into Toby's the other night I knew I had to go back. To find if three years had changed you, or if you still think you can stand apart from it all, as though it never happened.'

'You mean, don't you, that you want to convince yourself that you weren't mistaken. That there wasn't any doubt. That you needn't feel the slightest twinge of guilt about condemning me.'

'There wasn't much doubt about it.' Jordan's mouth compressed. 'We know Stuart was mentally off balance that night. He had a damned good reason. He thought you were going to marry him. Then he found that you were two-timing him with another man. Of course he was driving like a lunatic. What did you expect? That he'd just accept it? If he'd any sense he would have done,' Jordan added bitterly. 'He should have seen you for what you were—just another selfish, gold-digging little bitch.'

'You still believe that!' she whispered. 'Even though I told you why I was with Blaise that night, just after the——' She stopped, unable to go on, and Jordan's mouth twisted disbelievingly.

'You married Blaise, didn't you? I hope he had joy of his bargain.'

She shuddered convulsively under the cruel injustice of his scorn, and he said:

'There couldn't be any other explanation of your appalling behaviour, even leaving Blaise out of the picture. When you saw you couldn't evade the truth you were forced to admit that you'd been in the car with Stuart that night. And believe me, if that witness who saw you running away from the scene of the accident had been a bit more positive, I'd have seen to it that every headline in the country dragged your name through the mud and exposed you as the heartless little bitch you were. It was the least you deserved,' he added viciously. 'To leave him lying there like that, he could have died for all you cared. And then you tried to lie your way out of it.'

She recoiled from the disgust on his face. 'But it wasn't like that at all. I—I told you. Why wouldn't you believe me? I *did* go back! When it happened I—I .had to get help. I ran to find a phone box. It—it was miles away, and when I found it the phone was broken and—and I had to go on till I——'

'It was strange that there was no record of your making an emergency call, wasn't it?' he said sarcastically. 'Why do you waste your breath? We know what happened. That you were so damned scared you just ran like hell.'

'I didn't,' she whispered brokenly. 'I—I did go back, but by then it was too late.'

'You're damned right. It was too late.'

'But I told you. Somebody, it must have been that motorist—I don't know—phoned from a house. When —when I got back it was all over. Stuart had been taken to hospital. There was nothing I could do,' she repeated miserably.

'So you hurried back home and tried to pretend you knew nothing about it. And at first I believed you, even though your white face screamed the truth and your guilt. And then Stuart implored me to keep you out of it. He didn't want you involved in any enquiry. And for thanks you ditched him, walked out of his life, and married another man. And you wonder why I'm bitter!' he stormed.

Gerda's throat ached with the tears she dared not shed. She would never shake his conviction of her heartlessness, never be able to persuade him that the blame was not hers and never had been. Not unless she told him the whole truth. And she could never do that. It would bring too much pain into other lives. Pity had bought her silence, and as long as Stuart chose to remain silent so must she. But for how long must she go on reaping the agony of Jordan's bitter censure? Her hands clenched and she fought back her tears. If only he knew! If the slightest shred of guilt was hers she had paid for it in the cruellest way of all—by loving the one man who hated her and held her to blame.

Jordan said suddenly: 'If you'd been honest we wouldn't have blamed you so much. God knows, we're none of us saints, and the days are gone when a man expects a girl to be an angel—with the innocence of one. But it was that innocent look of yours, that you wore right from the start. If you'd said outright there was someone else, instead of stringing Stuart along. But you didn't. You even tried to pretend with me.'

Pretend!

'Oh no!' she cried with the involuntary force of pain. 'Blame me for Stuart's accident, if you must, but don't accuse me of pretending to *you*!'

'Didn't you?' He was very near her now, and his glance moved over her in a way that was almost insolent. 'That's not the way I remember it. Or was it that you couldn't make up your mind which of the two of us you wanted?'

His eyes were mesmerising her now, holding her bound to him as surely as if he had laid physical restraint on her. 'It shook Stuart that first weekend you came down here and said you didn't like messing about with boats. Sheer heresy. Stuart's girls always adored sailing and fast sports cars. They didn't choose to go walking and scrambling round the countryside with his brother.'

'You asked me to.'

He laughed shortly. 'I believed you. Some people are scared stiff on water. And being seasick simply to try to avoid spoiling the party wouldn't be my idea of an enjoyable weekend. So what else could I do but lay on alternative amusement? Such as it was,' he added dryly.

'You won't believe me, but I was grateful to you,' she said in a low voice. 'I had no idea when I accepted the invitation that Stuart intended to go sailing that weekend and that he expected me to go with him. I just couldn't.'

'And the nautical rig-out was just coincidence.'

She closed her eyes. He forgot nothing. Not even the clothes she wore, not even ... She shivered. 'It was the chance you had waited for, wasn't it? To check up on me. To judge if I was good enough for your young brother to marry.'

His brows arched. 'You had dress sense, I must admit. That little dark blue bikini thing with the white cords lacing it, and that white middy jacket with brass buttons and little red anchor ... no wonder Stuart was sceptical when you gave the boat the thumbs-down. It wasn't until later that I began to wonder.'

'No!' She turned blindly, knowing that he was determined to strip her soul bare, and knowing she must escape.

She snatched at her bag and scrambled to her feet, but with deceptive slowness Jordan also moved. He caught her arm and swung her to face him. Caught off balance, she stumbled and almost fell, but his grasp did not waver a fraction.

'You weren't in such a hurry the last time,' he observed coolly.

'Let me go!'

She tried to wrench free, and he shook his head. His mouth parted in a slight smile. 'Not yet.'

She stiffened as his hand curled round the nape of her neck and tangled in the thick soft tress of her hair, forcing her to look up at him.

'You're not eighteen and innocent any longer,

Gerda,' he said softly, and bent to her lips.

His mouth was hard and totally without tenderness, bruising the soft tenderness of hers, and with inexorable strength his arms curved her body to an arc against him. Her heart thumped as though it would burst and a dreadful weakness impaired the hopeless struggle to break free.

He raised his head and his eyes were half veiled under their lids. 'The first time I kissed you your mouth was as tight as a little closed purse and your body as rigid. Had you forgotten?'

She shuddered and turned blindly against his shoulder, beyond speech.

'That was the time when I really believed my judgement had gone haywire.' Jordan's voice was low and slumbrous against her hair. 'When we sat down here that afternoon and you flopped back, flushed and tired, and your hair still dark and wet with sea water, you looked so young and untouched I couldn't quite believe in you. That's why I kissed you to see if it was all real.'

He laughed softly, and went on scornfully: 'Do you know what I thought in those moments? I thought of your namesake in the old kids' storybook tale. And Kay with the Snow Queen's shaft of ice through his heart. I thought you had the ice of innocence in your heart. How mistaken can a man be?'

She moaned softly, and he pressed his hand under her chin, making her meet his gaze. 'I was on the point of drawing back, even framing words to warn you about my young brother's reputation with girls, and that was the moment you suddenly decided to give.'

Jordan paused, and his mouth curved in a mirthless smile of derision. 'I've never forgotten that moment when you slid one arm up round my shoulders and let

43

yourself go against me.'

Somewhere a sea-bird cried plaintively. It was like a sound from another world and Gerda shivered violently within the bonds of memory. His words had brought two levels of time into co-existence, and she burned, feeling as though her body was on fire against the long lean length of him. Jordan now, and Jordan then, a hot, sunlit afternoon, the tang of the sea on his skin, the roughness of sand clinging to her limbs, scraping under his hands. . . .

How could she ever convince him that he had been the first man ever to lay hands on her body, those first wild caresses that ran from shoulder to thigh, to rest in the concave hollow of her spine. *'I've always liked girls to be long-limbed and slender, but smooth and not bony. . . .'* His words and his kiss and his caress had merged into an ecstacy that swept all her resistance before it, like the bursting of floodgates before the onslaught of the flood, and for the first time in her eighteen summers she had known what it meant to be alive in every tingling sense, and in love. . . .

Jordan's hands fell away from her, and she experienced the same deathly sense of loss, as though part of her had suddenly ceased to live. He said slowly: 'I wondered how many men you'd fooled with that wide-eyed look, that ice in the heart, kidding them along until they lost their heads over you.'

She turned away, her shoulders bowed with defeat. 'You know it all, don't you?' she said bitterly.

'I do now.' His tone was rough with disgust. 'I didn't know then about the calendar business, that Stuart had picked himself a cheap little pin-up model. If I'd known then things would have taken a totally different course, I can assure you of that.'

'You wouldn't have demeaned yourself to make love

44

to your brother's girl, I suppose,' she flung at him.

'You wouldn't have been my brother's girl.'

'I wish you had known! I wish I'd never met you. Nothing will ever make you believe me, you're determined to believe the worst of me without a shred of evidence to prove it.' Her voice choked, and suddenly even pride no longer mattered. 'You were the first man who'd ever kissed me like that. So whatever you think I am, you helped to make me.'

'Me? A couple of kisses? Oh, Gerda, it's a bit late in the day for that kind of pretence.'

'But it's true,' she said vehemently, 'and I hated you that day, almost as much as I hated myself.'

'Hate?' He gave an exclamation of disbelief. 'Because I tried to make love to you?'

'Yes. Because I was fool enough to believe you meant it.'

He looked down at her, unmoved by the glisten of angry tears in her eyes. 'What did you expect, for heaven's sake? A girl lies in a man's arms and clings to him. And then you got scared. You remembered that you weren't wearing much in the way of clothes to get in the way and you put on a fine show of outraged modesty.'

He stroked his cheek and regarded her with cool, insolent eyes. 'It wasn't a very convincing slap, really.'

Involuntarily she clenched her hand. It tingled, as though that slap still echoed on the air, and she fought for control, for strength to fight him, wishing she could hurt him a fraction of the way he had hurt her. But the impulse died as quickly as it came. He was impervious to wounding—or to any appeal to his mercy.

She turned away. 'Well, what now? Are you satisfied? Do you want me to go back and tell Charingfolds they've had it? That the contract goes to their rivals?

Go on!' Abruptly she whirled to face him. 'Why don't you say it? You have no intention of giving us that contract.'

'But I've said no such thing.'

'Maybe not, but it's obvious all the same.'

Jordan's expression did not change. He bent and picked up the jerkin, then faced her. 'Durrel hasn't taught you much about the business side of life, has he?'

'I don't know what you mean by that,' she returned, 'but I know enough to trust my own instincts.'

'And what do they tell you?' His tone was loaded with meaning.

'That I'm wasting my time,' she said hotly. 'And *you* are wasting yours.'

'So I'm wasting my time.' The lazy drawl had returned. He jumped down lithely and held up his hand. 'In what way?'

She avoided his hand and stumbled down the little ridge on to the shingle. 'Because it's all pointless. It's all over.'

'What's all over?' He seemed to be taking a delight in pinning down her wild, vague retorts.

'Everything. And you know it as well as I do.'

'Do I?' He stared down into her distraught face, then shook his head. 'I don't think so.' He raised one hand and stroked it almost caressingly down her cheek. 'It isn't over, Gerda. It's just beginning.'

CHAPTER III

THE passing years had brought little visible change to Green Rigg and its environs. Despite the widening of the coast road less than half a mile away, the rambling old manor still held an air of being untouched by the race of modern progress, as though the green hollow in which it nestled had been bypassed and forgotten for another century.

The golden haze of the evening sun mellowed the scarlet creeper that curtained the gable and washed the diamond-paned windows with liquid gold as the car rounded the curve and entered the drive gates. The gentle peace of it all only seemed to heighten the sense of foreboding that lay over Gerda's spirit, and she was shocked to find that her limbs were actually trembling when she got out of the car. Suddenly she wished with all her heart she'd been elsewhere when Jordan came to the flat that morning, wished she'd had the strength of mind to refuse to fall in with the arrangements he'd forced her to accept.

He walked round the front of the car and his long shadow merged with her own. He tucked one hand under her elbow with apparent casualness and walked her towards the side of the house. She tried not to shiver; it might have been three years back in time, with Stuart's hand tucked in hers, leading her to the garden door which everyone seemed to use.

The big sun-room was exactly the same; deep comfortable chairs and faded chintz, the worn green ping-pong table near the window, the pieces of furniture that didn't match yet seemed to blend in the one room in the house that was for relaxing in. Books lay about, and the big blue jar still stood on a small cabinet in one corner, peony roses shedding their petals around it. Gerda wondered inconsequently if Jordan's mother was still as house-proud. Every other room in the house was polished and matched and beautiful, with that silence and atmosphere that made one move stiffly and carefully if left alone amid Mrs Black's treasures. Perhaps it was different now, she thought as Jordan walked straight through the long room and into a narrow white-painted hall she didn't remember.

'We've made quite a few alterations since you were last here,' Jordan remarked, swinging her weekend case lightly as he led the way. 'This is my part of the house now. We had to make adjustments because of Stuart. Naturally, stairs are impossible for him, so we turned the ground floor of the west wing into his apartments. My mother has the original drawing room and the suite above Stuart's. We find it all works better that way.'

He paused at the head of the stairs and gestured towards the door at the right. 'Make yourself at home. There's about an hour before dinner. Come down when you're ready—I'll be next door to the sun-room.'

He held out the case and she took it wordlessly, hesitating until he should turn back to the stairway. But he didn't move, merely looked at her from under raised brows. 'Well, go on. Or do you want me to come and unpack for you?'

Her expression closed. 'That won't be necessary.' Abruptly she thrust open the door of the guest room and shut it behind her with unnecessary force. For a few moments, so casual and laconic had been his manner, a brief sense of normality had returned to her and she had begun almost to believe that this was just another country weekend visit and she was just another arrival casually blown in.

But she wasn't, and it was going to be a far from casual country weekend.

For one thing the whole place seemed utterly deserted. She dropped her case on the bed and crossed to the window. Both casements were open to the soft mild breeze that was blowing from inland, and she rested her hands on the windowsill while she looked out across the grounds beneath. She was facing the front of the house, the smooth velvet-green lawns and the banks of hydrangeas, and the deeper metallic green of the Mercedes still stood on the left-hand sweep of the drive below. Gerda frowned, staring a moment longer at the deserted vista before she turned back to the room and quickly unpacked her few things. A sense of reluctance stayed with her as she hung them in the big white fitted wardrobe and set her personal toiletries on the glass-topped dressing table. Through the mirror her eyes were shadowed and uncertain, and she looked away quickly, trying to shake off unease as she applied milky cleanser.

It was only for little over twenty-four hours. She mustn't lose her nerve like this. Mustn't let Jordan see she was afraid of him. Why should she be afraid of him? she asked herself in a feverish attempt to reason with herself. Face facts. He hated her, blamed her, and he had power to hurt her. To hurt her through denying Howard the contract, to hurt her because she ...

Gerda closed her mind to the real reason she dared not face. No, it was over. After three years she wasn't going to allow him the satisfaction of knowing how much he could disturb her peace of mind. With a shudder she turned away from the betrayal of her own frightened eyes in the mirror. She would never know peace of mind until she was as far away as she could get from Jordan Black.

Her outward appearance of calm was a frail, hard-won façade when she went downstairs and retraced her steps. She still hadn't seen or heard a trace of anyone else in the house and the dark thoughts were still trying to invade her, like a faceless thing from the dark that sought to overpower her. So it was with a sudden sense of relief that she heard the raised voice of a girl from the half-open door of the room next to the sun-room.

Gerda stopped, and the voice stopped. Then she heard Jordan snap: 'No. We're dining with him to-night, so you'll have to forget it.'

'But I've arranged it.' The voice sounded sulky. 'He wanted to. It was his idea.'

'I don't care a damn whose idea it was. You're not taking Stuart along to the Merrivale tonight, so you can——'

'Can I? Well, for once *you* can forget it!' The young voice rose with anger. 'It's always the same. You'd give anything if you could get rid of me, wouldn't you, Jordan Black? You're terrified in case I take him away from you. You've always wanted to manage his life and keep him under your thumb. Well, it won't work this time, do you hear! And I think you're a heartless wretch to bring *her* back after the way she let him down. He doesn't want her! He doesn't love her any more. He loves *me*! And you're not going to stop him. I——'

'Shut up. If you can't behave yourself for once, then get out.'

'I won't. How dare you talk to me like that! You——'

50

'I'll talk to you any way I want. Now for heaven's sake stop talking like a stupid little adolescent. You have the whole week to amuse yourself and Stuart, is it asking too much to respect my wishes for one evening?'

'Wishes! You're more like a dictator. You——'

'Maybe.' Jordan's tone held the chill of ice. 'Tell Leon I want him.'

'I'm not a servant!'

'If you don't like it you know what to do.'

There was a gasp, then running feet and an angry exclamation. The girl appeared, oval face white against a scarlet slash of lipstick and jet-black hair flowing wildly. She was almost in tears and she stopped short, her dark eyes widening as she almost collided with Gerda. For a moment she stared at the older girl, then Jordan's dark-clad form appeared at the doorway and with a look of hatred at him and Gerda she brushed past and fled down the hall.

Jordan's features were hard with anger and his voice rigidly controlled as he gestured brusquely for Gerda to enter. An instinctive feeling of sympathy for anyone who fell foul of Jordan's ire was being replaced by incredulous realisation.

He started to speak and she broke in: 'Is that ... was that Rachel Lammond? The——'

'Sir Hubert's daughter? Yes.' Jordan shot her a sharp look. 'Do you know her?'

'No—that is I once met her very briefly, years ago.' Gerda looked away. 'I wasn't sure if it was her,' she said carefully.

'It's Rachel all right, the spoilt little bitch. She's as neurotic as hell now at eighteen. God knows what she'll be like in a few years' time,' he said brutally. 'Excuse me, I'll be back in a second.'

With the murmured aside he was hurrying out, leav-

51

ing Gerda thankful for the unexpected respite in which to grapple with this fresh shock. What on earth was Rachel Lammond doing here?

Gerda sank into a chair and stared unseeingly at the book-lined, mannish room. Rachel's father was the former chairman of the Wentford Combine and still a formidable figure in the financial world. Years ago there had been bitter enmity between Sir Hubert and Arnold Black, Jordan's father. Sir Hubert had twice thwarted Arnold Black's attempts at expansion in the widening field of electronics and Arnold had retaliated by undercutting so drastically he had all but beggared his own firm. Now Arnold was dead, Sir Hubert had retired well content, and Jordan Black was the man in power at Wentford. Just how he had accomplished the series of lightning coups which had brought him to power in the camp of his father's old enemy Gerda did not know, but achieve them he had, and, if Howard's prediction proved right, the chairmanship would be his within a year.

Had it been for the motive of revenge? Gerda wondered. He was ruthless, certainly, but she was forced to admit he had little cause to be sympathetic to the memory of Sir Hubert's former glory.

So where did Rachel fit in?

Judging by the wild way she had defied him, and the way he had spoken to, and of her, the old enmity had lived on. Gerda got up and paced to the window, her heart like a leaden weight in her breast. Surely Stuart wasn't encouraging her to defy his brother; in that way lay danger and fresh heartbreak.

She closed her eyes despairingly. What had happened during those three years when she had succeeded in freeing herself from the dark influence of the Black family? Was she to be dragged back helplessly

52

into their stormy lives?

The moments of troubled reflection masked the almost soundless movements of Jordan coming back into the room. She gave a gasp as his hands fell on her shoulders and he said softly: 'Didn't you hear me come in?'

'No.' She edged smoothly to one side so that his hands slid away. 'Do you always creep up on people like that?'

'Only when they go off into a daydream.' He looked at her rather closely. 'What's the matter? You look sorry for yourself.'

She made herself return his stare steadily and shook her head. 'I gave up being sorry for myself a long time ago—and that was the day I grew up.'

'It must have been a sad day.'

She shrugged, and he smiled slightly, with that characteristic narrowing of his eyes. 'You're not sorry for me?'

'You are the last person I'd be sorry for.' Her mouth was hard. She turned away. 'Are you looking for sympathy?'

'I never look for sympathy.'

'You never give it, either.'

'But I do, my dear Gerda.' He was mixing drinks somewhere behind her. 'Always remembering that at its best sympathy is but a fleeting anodyne and at its worst a maudlin wallow. Do you still play safe with sherry?' he added without the slightest variation in his tone.

'It depends on how long I have to play safe,' she returned. 'Where's Stuart?'

'Changing for dinner, I expect—in your honour.' Jordan held out her drink. 'In view of that little scene just now I've packed Rachel off for the evening.'

'And she went?'

He nodded and leaned against the mantelshelf, studying the clarity of the wine in his glass before he took it to his lips.

Just like that! Gerda sighed and remained by the window. From the little she had known and heard of Rachel it was difficult to imagine her being so instantly tractable. Still less if she'd been curtly told to cancel arrangements already made.

'Leon's gone with her,' Jordan went on casually. 'I thought it would be easier to talk if there was just the three of us.'

Would it? She looked into her glass but made no move to drink. 'Who's Leon?'

'He looks after Stuart. There has to be someone to lift him in and out of his chair, help him to dress, help him to——'

'Yes—I realise. I—I should have ...' Gerda's eyes filled with pain and her mouth trembled. 'I'm sorry. It—it must be dreadful for him.' She sank down on the window seat, suddenly realising how much she dreaded the coming meeting with Stuart Black. What good could it do? she wondered hopelessly. She'd be the last person the crippled boy wanted to see. If only she knew what dark deviousness Jordan was planning....

'You need that drink.' He loomed over her, his eyes compelling her to look up at him. 'Go on, drink it.'

As she made a mechanical move to obey he sat down at her side. 'Are you really afraid of seeing Stuart again?' he asked softly.

'No—not seeing him. You make it sound as though I were afraid of—of facing something repulsive when you say it like that.' She tried to evade his intent gaze. 'It isn't that. It—it's not that at all.'

'Then what is it?'

'Is it wise? What will it achieve? How is it going to help Stuart?' Her control wavered and she reached out, almost to touch him before she checked the gesture. 'Jordan, are you sure you're doing the right thing in starting this all over again? It's all past. It can't be undone. It can't be changed.'

'No, it can't be any of those things. But I thought I'd made it clear this afternoon. Or have you forgotten already?'

'I've forgotten nothing,' she said wearily.

'Then surely you'll agree; it's time to start bringing it to an end.'

'An end?'

'Yes.' He took her unresisting hands and drew her to her feet. 'You seem unable to grasp one very simple fact, Gerda. You can't start forgetting anything until it ends.'

He stayed motionless, looking down into her troubled face, then he touched her cheek with the same caressing gesture he had used earlier that afternoon.

'Come, Gerda,' he said suavely. 'It's time I took you to Stuart.'

• • •

As Jordan silently escorted her to the other part of the house Gerda tensed and wondered what she was going to say to Stuart during those first difficult moments of the meeting. Suddenly she wondered if Jordan had warned his brother that he was bringing her. It would be typical of Jordan's twisted humour to spring a surprise on Stuart. She shivered; the thought held an element of sadism. Surely Jordan wouldn't ... But Stuart might not even recognise her. Three years was quite a time; they'd changed her. But of course he would know her. He . . .

When Jordan stopped and the door swung open at his touch she hung back. Her mouth felt dry, as though the prepared words of greeting would stick in her throat, then Jordan gave her a light push and his touch under her shoulder-blade sent her forward. She took in the big room, the wheelchair facing the french window, and her wild notion of an incredulous, confused exchange of greetings fled. It wasn't going to be like that.

The chair wheeled round and Stuart said sulkily: 'You've taken your time. Where the hell have you been?'

For a moment she thought he meant her, until Jordan stepped forward. 'Dealing with your precocious girl-friend—you're encouraging trouble there. Now, if you can't be pleasant, Stuart, try to be polite.'

'Am I not? Hello, Gerda darling. Long time no see.'

She felt numbed, her automatic response stilted and unreal.

Jordan said: 'Fix her a drink. I'll see you at dinner.'

Abruptly he withdrew without even a glance at her, and she stood uncertainly, meeting the dark ironic gaze so disconcertingly like Jordan's. She took a step forward, trying to smile, and Stuart said sharply: 'Oh, for God's sake . . . not you as well!'

He held out his hands and gave a twisted smile at her shocked expression. 'You're just the same as the rest of them. If they haven't seen me since it happened. They try not to look at this'—he flapped one hand over the light grey quilted silk covering over his knees—'and not think of my useless legs underneath, and they force bright smiles and ask me how I am. They make me sick!'

'I'm sure they don't intend to,' she said awkwardly. 'I

won't ask how you are, then.'

'You'd better not. I prefer to be ignored.'

'Wouldn't that be callous?' She wanted to define his meaning as ignoring of his disability, but dared not.

He shrugged. 'Do you want that drink?'

'Not really.' She looked away, aware of an immeasurable distance in time and understanding between them and unsure how to cross it without guidance from him. 'What a lovely room.'

'It's not bad. Is that all you can say?'

She bit her lip. 'I don't know what to say, or what you want me to say. It's been such a long time, Stuart.'

'Yes. Too long.' His intent gaze was rather unnerving. 'I wish you'd come over here. You know I can't come to you.'

Slowly, she approached, feeling her eyes smarting despite the trace of ungraciousness in his voice. Stuart was still moody and petulant, but his illness had made little change in his facial appearance. A shadow was catching him and his resemblance to his brother was uncanny. He was still the boyishly immature edition of Jordan; the same lean clear-cut features, smooth, olive-dark skin, the same characteristic jut of the sensuously full lower lip, and his eyes were startlingly like Jordan's under their black fringes of lashes. Only the hair struck the abruptly different note. Stuart's was black, thick and springy, and tending to curl, and his chinline was softer, not so pronounced, and when he was sitting the slightness of his frame in comparison to Jordan's broad-shouldered strength was not so apparent.

'That's better,' he said, flashing an impudent grin. 'You can approach with perfect safety now, you know. I couldn't seduce you—even if I wanted to.'

She smiled faintly. 'We're older and wiser now.'

His grin faded. He held out one hand and she took

57

it, letting hers rest in the warm enclosing grasp. 'Older, but not wiser. I've just realised how much I've missed you.'

'Have you? I've often thought of you. Wondered how you were.' She glanced over his head but did not really see the cool soft colours of the garden. 'Sometimes I was tempted to write, but in the circumstances...' She let her voice trail into silence.

'Why didn't you?'

She made no reply and he tightened his grip on her hand. 'Why didn't you come back to see me in hospital?'

'I didn't think you wanted me to.'

His expression became thoughtful, then perceptive. 'Sure Jordan didn't scare you off?'

'No.' It was a lie, but she did not want to retread the dangerous path it could bare. 'I thought it was better if I didn't.'

Again he was silent, that perceptive glance alert. Then he gave a twisted smile. 'No, I suppose you were wise.'

She thought of Jordan and the bitterness of memory welled again. Her instincts and her motives during those dreadful days might have been many things, but the least of them had been wisdom. Now it was too late for anything but regret.

He said suddenly: 'Have you forgiven me yet?'

'Of course. I forgave you a long time ago—not that there was anything to forgive. There wasn't.'

'I'm glad.' He was searching her face, holding tight to her hand. 'I've forgiven you as well.'

'That makes two of us then.' The words were meant to be light, but they sounded feeble to her own ears. 'I wish...' she began, and stopped, shaking her head.

'Wish it had never happened?'

'Yes, oh yes.' How could she tell him she wished also to hear words of forgiveness from Jordan's lips? She sighed, knowing she might as well wish for the moon, and Stuart made a small tugging movement at her hand.

'Come back from wherever you went just then and cheer up. I'm glad you came today,' he added softly.

She smiled and made the obvious response, moving to look out at the attractively landscaped garden. 'It's wonderful to get out of the city when the weather's so gorgeous. I notice there are no steps out there. You'll be able to spend a lot of time outdoors when it's fine.'

'Yes. Haven't you got anything else for the invalid?'

She started, not having heard the silent movement of the chair, and looked down at him. His raised brows and wry expression made his meaning perfectly clear, and she stooped to give him the kiss he wanted. Abruptly he reached up and locked his hands round the back of her head, holding her down to him with all his old strength.

His kiss was long and searching and deliberate, and his soft sigh inquisitive, as though he sought to stir a fiery response in her as ardently as once he had so vainly tried. Her heart contracted, and compassion tempted her to instil a response she did not feel. But she checked the unwise prompting of pity, knowing the unfairness of it even if he did not, and drew back. Slowly he let his hands slide loose, to catch at her face and frame it for a moment before he released her.

'You haven't changed, Gerda,' he said slowly. 'You look different, more sure of yourself and much more beautiful, but inside you're still the same. Still cool, and self-sufficient, and still afraid to let yourself go. Do you know,' he relaxed back and allowed her to straighten, 'you were the first girl who succeeded in holding out against me.'

'Surely not.' She drew a stool to the side of his chair and sat down, trying to keep her tone light. 'Surely I wasn't the only girl in your life.'

'You were the only girl who wouldn't sleep with me,' he said flatly.

'You had a persuasive way with you,' she returned.

'But it wasn't persuasive enough. Why do you think I asked you to marry me?' He looked at her from the corners of his eyes in a way she remembered very well, and his mouth quirked cynically. 'You were the classic proof of the old-fashioned way of winning a man.'

'Was that the only reason for your proposal?'

'No,' his head tilted to one side, 'not entirely. Even though I was mad because you were using the old blackmail——'

'I wasn't!'

'Weren't you? Marry me or nothing doing!' He assumed a dramatic expression, then sobered abruptly. 'But you were still the only girl I'd met whom I felt I could stand waking up to every morning for the rest of my life.'

'So you intended it to be permanent?' She felt a sense of relief that they could be light-hearted now, so long afterwards.

'As permanent as anything could be in this day and age.'

'But I never thought of it as blackmailing you into proposing marriage—honestly,' she said, the old defensiveness returning.

'No? You just led me along like a will-o'-the-wisp.' Stuart laughed and touched something at the side of his chair. It swung round and glided so swiftly and silently that again she was unprepared for the movement. In the centre of the big room he stopped and looked round at her. 'Come on, I'll show you all the gadgets. I'm not entirely helpless, you know.'

She stood up and crossed the empty central expanse. 'I can see that. You can get round quicker than I can.'

'Sometimes I chase Rachel.' He laughed shortly, his mood perceptibly altering. 'I kid her I'm going to run her down. One day I nearly did.'

'I'm not surprised,' she said dryly. On the special composition surface of the floor the wheelchair had a smooth turn of speed that was deceptive, and she could well imagine Stuart indulging in a macabre skylarking that would assuage the bitterness of his disability.

As though he guessed at her thoughts he grinned. 'It's the sadist in me. A kind of twisted superiority complex. I have to prove to myself that I can still dominate people even though I can't walk.'

She stayed silent, following as he skimmed towards the other door at the far end of the room. When the chair was about three feet away from it the door swung open, then closed silently, almost trapping Gerda before she got through.

'Sorry—I should have warned you. There's a device that motivates it,' he explained, halting and waving his hand to indicate the room in general. 'See, there's a panel here beside the bed. From it I can control my radio and television, the heating and air-conditioning, and the lighting. I can open the windows, swing this bookcase into reach, and ring for Leon or the servants.'

'An electronic miracle,' she commented. 'What's this one for?'

He touched the switch in question and immediately the shades slid down over the windows, plunging the room into dimness, and a small pilot light glowed over another switch. 'Then I put on whatever light I want, wherever I want.'

She glanced at the wall screen, the stereophonic recording equipment, the miniature cocktail bar with sliding shutters above that was built into the dividing wall so that it could be used in both rooms of the suite, and the luxurious fittings of cream leather and parana pine against lime green and touches of vivid orange. Everything that money and ingenuity could supply had gone into Stuart's suite; but how could it ever compensate ...?

Watching her, he chuckled softly. 'Sordid opulence, isn't it?'

'Someone gave a great deal of thought to all this,' she said soberly.

He chuckled again. 'Power at my fingertips. All by courtesy of my benevolent big brother.'

'Did he have all this installed?' She blinked as the lights died and the shades folded, letting the strong gold rays of the setting sun reach back into the room.

'Yes. He had a couple of experts down to help him work it all out. They forgot nothing—except a couple of gadgets I could use for legs.'

He returned into the other room and made for the window, waiting until she caught up with him and sat down on the red stool. He seemed to be waiting for some comment from her, and at last she said slowly: 'Can't they do anything, Stuart?'

'For me, you mean?'

She nodded, already wondering if the question was wise.

'No. I saw a procession of them. Surgeons, osteopaths—even a faith healer,' he interjected scornfully. 'They all said the same: there's no life in the nerves and it's hopeless to attempt repairing the damage. Until last year.' Stuart paused to offer and light a cigarette for her, reaching for an ashtray before she had time to spot one and fetch it. 'Last year Jordan heard of a German specialist with a tremendous skill for treating apparently hopeless cases. So he flew me over there to see this surgeon.'

'Yes ...?' she prompted when he hesitated.

Stuart's mouth had set in hard lines and it was some time before he gave a resigned gesture. 'I suppose he was the first one to hold out a ray of hope. He was willing to operate, but the chance wasn't even fifty-fifty. He offered a three in one chance that I'd regain the use of my legs again.'

'And you didn't take it?'

'Do you take me for a fool? There were far too many reservations.' Stuart dragged angrily on his cigarette. 'I might walk again. It *might* be on sticks. There might be lack of co-ordination. *Might!*' he said bitterly. 'Might not.'

'But there's always an element of uncertainty,' she said earnestly. 'There was a time when my mother was so ill it looked terribly dark, but today she's wonderful, happier than she's ever been in her life.'

'No doubt.' Stuart gave a sigh. 'But in this case it was having to make the choice. You see, he warned me it might be curtains altogether. Would *you* risk it?'

'I don't know,' she said slowly, wondering how she would make so agonising a decision if it were hers to make. 'I don't know,' she repeated. 'I think I might if ... Yes, I think it would be worth anything if there was a chance.'

'To walk or to die?'

She looked away.

'No, thanks. My mother didn't want me to risk it, in spite of Jordan, and that was enough for me. It's all very well for him to talk of this being a living death, but he hasn't got to take the awful chance. Yes, this made me see that it wasn't quite as bad as I'd imagined,' he added wryly. 'Until last year life was hellish—and I made sure it was hell for everybody else. But after the German trip and I'd had time to reflect, I decided I didn't want to die, after all, and that there was a certain small satisfaction in being able to manipulate the strings. And now I've got you back.'

'You sound like a puppet-master.'

'Do I? Wishful thinking—again by courtesy of Big Brother. He, my dear Gerda, is the big manipulator round here.'

Again she was silent, wondering at the bitterness in his voice when he spoke of Jordan. When she first knew the brothers there had been a certain amount of antipathy sensed between them, but she assumed it to be the normal antagonism often found between brothers when the oldest was the more ruthless and dominant and the younger one spoilt and with a tendency to wildness. But now . . .

She was aware of relief when the door opened at that moment and Jordan appeared. However, Stuart did not appear to share her feeling. He looked round at the tall figure in the immaculate dark suit and said sulkily: 'What do you want? We're getting on fine without any supervision.'

'It's time to eat,' Jordan said calmly. 'Or aren't you bothered?'

He seemed unmoved by Stuart's rudeness. Or was it that he was immune to the moods and surliness of the crippled boy? All the same he showed remarkable control and patience, far more than she would have credited him with when she thought of his attitude towards herself, Gerda reflected sadly as she went with the two brothers to the dining room.

She could not say that the atmosphere was exactly

enjoyable during the otherwise pleasant meal in the oak-beamed room overlooking the terrace at the front of the house. There was a marked air of restraint that did not lessen after the housekeeper brought in the delicious asparagus soup and then withdrew, leaving them to help themselves to a ham mousse and huge bouquet salad when they were ready.

Jordan was excessively urbane during the meal, or so it seemed to Gerda, and she found it more disturbing than his cold aggressiveness. Stuart made little attempt to keep the conversation going. In one respect he had not altered, she thought; he still betrayed every mood transparently, making no effort to disguise his inward resentment when anything upset him or someone crossed a particular whim of the moment. It came as a relief when he crumpled his napkin and flung it on the lower shelf of the serving trolley. He looked at Jordan.

'I think you might have let me know a bit sooner.'

'What about?'

'About this weekend. And Gerda.'

'I let you know last night. Isn't that soon enough?' Jordan's calm was unbroken as he helped Gerda to a serving of rainbow dessert, trying to persuade her to take a much larger portion than she wanted. 'You must have some cream with it—it's from the farm. You, Stuart?'

'No, thanks.' Stuart reached for the coffee pot. 'You've got a nerve. You haven't shown your nose here for six weeks, or even phoned, then you suddenly appear with Gerda. Why didn't you tell me?'

'I didn't know myself.'

And neither did I—till nearly lunchtime today! she thought with a flash of anger. So he had decided last night; how sure he must have been that she would acquiesce. But then he knew he held the whip hand.

65

Stuart was saying: 'Of course it wouldn't strike you that Rachel might have planned out our whole weekend.'

'As a matter of fact, it did,' Jordan said smoothly. 'So don't concern yourself.' A hint of sarcasm crept into his tone at last. 'We'll fall in with whatever plans have been made, and if *that* doesn't suit I'll merely take Gerda back to town tomorrow morning and we'll discuss our business there.'

'Business?' Stuart was shaken out of his pet. 'What business?'

'A contract. Gerda's with Charingfolds now.'

'You didn't tell me.' Stuart's accusing glance encompassed Gerda as well as his brother. 'I thought you'd just bumped into her and asked her down for—for old times' sake.'

'You thought wrong, then.'

'It seems I usually do.' Stuart glared. 'Supposing you consult——'

'Please!' Gerda couldn't stand any more. 'For heaven's sake, stop wrangling! *I* had no intention of upsetting your weekend, and if—if I'd known I——'

Jordan's hand closed over her knee, unseen under cover of the table. 'Let me settle this. You're not upsetting anything. If——'

'Darling, I didn't mean you!' Stuart interrupted. 'I——'

'—if you'll let us know what you *do* want,' Jordan went on inexorably, showing signs of losing patience, 'we can settle the matter. Shall we depart and leave you to amuse yourself as planned?' His grasp tightened momentarily, then slid away.

'If you only brought her to talk business you might as well,' Stuart grumbled. 'The crowd's coming over in the morning and we're all going up the river for a

66

barbecue, then we're going to wind up at the Black Linnet. It'll be quite a party.'

'Then we'll join it,' said Jordan calmly.

'Carrying your briefcase?' Stuart sniggered.

Jordan chose to ignore this, but Gerda could not help thinking it boded ill for the following day. She felt the dawning of reluctant sympathy for Jordan. It was obvious he had done everything humanly possible to alleviate his brother's tragedy and that he was genuinely devoted to him, but it was equally obvious that Stuart took full advantage of this. During the following day it soon became apparent that Jordan was not the only one over whom Stuart wielded the full influence that human sympathy and affection made possible.

Potentate was the word which occurred to Gerda when the Sunday party got under full way. From his wheelchair Stuart reigned. His was the noisiest voice, his personality the most dominant, he it was who cut short a topic or extended a pursuit. When Stuart got bored with a particular place everyone packed into the cars and moved on to the next spot on the route; when Stuart suddenly decided it was time to call it a day and go home to start a poker school they all went back to Green Rigg and played poker.

Gerda couldn't play. She had never been a keen card player and the dimly recalled childhood games of Beggar-my-neighbour and Rummy seemed poor practice for a poker school with the gay, sophisticated young crowd gathered round Stuart.

'Sit out and watch for a bit,' suggested Rachel, taking her place next to Stuart and making sure he had cigarettes, lighter, ashtray, and his drink to hand. 'Shall I put the new tape on, darling?' she asked, turning to him.

'Yes, good idea, and Gerda can sit beside me. I'll play her hand for her until she's got the hang of it. Is Leon getting the drinks flowing?'

Leon was already bringing the black and silver trolley to within convenient reach of the oval table round which the players were shuffling their chairs into place. He was much younger than Gerda had expected him to be, quiet, fair-haired, and slender, deceptively so, when she considered the ease with which he lifted Stuart from his chair into the car. He had been with Stuart for nearly two years as companion and masseur-therapist, and it was clear the two had become close friends.

But Rachel was the puzzling element, Gerda thought as the cards were dealt and the game began. There was something strangely erratic in her attitude to the two brothers. She was almost possessive towards Stuart, rarely straying from his side, but she seemed completely to forget her earlier exhibition of antagonism towards Jordan as the day wore on. Once she drew him aside, to engage him in earnest conversation. She seemed concerned, as though she were seeking something from him, but whether it was advice, confirmation, or reassurance it was difficult to tell, and judging by her expression she had received no satisfaction from whatever Jordan said to her before he brushed her away with that curt indifference which could wound so readily. Rachel had been quiet after the small incident, lying in the sun at Stuart's side with her face hidden in her hands while the others fooled about in the water. However, her volatile nature had soon recovered and now she still betrayed no animosity to Jordan as the game of cards got under way—on the contrary, she was almost flirtatious.

He and Stuart—who was still playing Gerda's hand —were the last two still in the round, and Rachel got up to go and stand behind Jordan, leaning on his shoulder so that she could watch his hand. In contrast to his impassive expression hers was alight and her dark eyes were sparkling with glee. She leaned closer, putting her lips against his ear, and whispered something, but Jordan neither moved nor gave the slightest indication of having heard.

'He'll turn round and wring her neck in a moment, the silly little idiot,' Stuart remarked to Gerda. 'The look on her face is enough to tell us the strength of his hand.'

He looked across at his brother and grinned. 'I'll see you.' Then he groaned and flung down his cards. 'Thanks, darling!' he cried to Rachel, 'I'd have gone to the skies on those queens.'

'We had the kings, didn't we?' Rachel's small slender fingers curved round Jordan's shoulder. 'I brought you luck, didn't I?'

'Did you?' The slight lift of his brows was enigmatic. 'I'd better chalk it up to you—you can take over my hand.'

He stood up and held the chair for her, his light pressure on her arm making it difficult for her to do otherwise than obey, then he strolled to the other end of the table and looked down at his brother.

'You can count Gerda out as well—she'll never make a poker player.' He put both hands lightly on her shoulders as he spoke.

'Do you mind?' Stuart said mockingly.

'Not in the least.' As though he hadn't the slightest doubt that she would comply with his oblique command Jordan waited until she rose and then turned away with a laconic 'Goodnight' to the company.

She looked wordlessly at him as he closed the door behind them, already beginning to despise herself for obeying so meekly. He grinned. 'Think of the stakes I'm saving you—anyway, you weren't enjoying it very much, were you?'

'Not really,' she admitted unwillingly.

'Good. I dislike seeing women gaming.'

'But it was just a friendly game,' she observed as he motioned her into his study. 'They were only playing for small stakes.'

'Don't kid yourself. They'll be there till the small hours, and a couple of hundred quid will have changed hands—with those small stakes. Could you afford to lose a couple of hundred tonight?'

'You sound as though you were rescuing me from a gambling hell—in your own house,' she said lightly.

His laugh was an instant disillusionment. 'I'm not rescuing you from anything, my dear. I want to talk to you.'

The shell of wariness closed round her again. She watched him mix drinks, and when he put the ice-cold glass into her hand she could not repress a tremor. She looked up at the dark face and wondered if she imagined a hint of calculation in the slight smile on his mouth. 'The contract ...?'

'Later.'

He flipped open a box of the cigarettes he had specially blended at Morlands for himself and offered it to her. When she shook her head he closed the lid without taking a cigarette himself and picked up his drink. For a moment he nursed the glass reflectively, then glanced up sharply at her.

'What do you think of Stuart's crowd?'

She stared, taken aback by the unexpected question. 'They—they're all right. Good fun—if you want gay company.'

'You weren't impressed.'

70

'I didn't say that. Why do you ask me? It isn't for me to air my opinion.'

'I wanted to know it.'

She had sensed it had been no casual question, uttered merely for the sake of saying something, and she gave a small negative gesture. 'But why mine?'

Jordan ignored the puzzlement in her gesture. He drained his glass and set it down on the glass table, making a hollow musical ring that sounded oddly loud in the stillness. 'What did you think of Rachel?'

Again she felt the kick of surprise, this time with a definite impact of warning. She said slowly: 'What are you getting at, Jordan? You sound as though you're trying to find confirmation of some suspicion of your own.'

'I'm not asking for the fun of it,' he said coldly, 'but I certainly don't need confirmation of what I know.'

There was something in his eyes that worried her, and a sudden rush of foreboding made her feel sick. What did he know? Had Stuart——? But that was impossible. If Stuart——

'I should have put it this way,' Jordan went on, 'and asked if you'd formed any impression of Rachel's relationship to my brother.'

'She seems very fond of him,' Gerda said carefully. 'But how can I judge from one day? And'—she hesitated, feeling as though she were groping in darkness—'what is there to judge? Stuart needs young company. It must be dreadful for him.'

'Yes, but he doesn't need Rachel's.'

'You don't like her, do you?' she said flatly.

'She's the worst possible influence on him. Even worse than my mother.'

Gerda was shocked at the vehemence in his voice. 'You can't mean that seriously,' she protested. 'How

71

could anyone influence him adversely?'

'How?' Jordan laughed bitterly. 'Every weekend the house fills with those crazy kids—half the week as well at times. They drink and gamble and go wild, and Rachel was the one who brought them.'

'But he has to have companionship,' she repeated. 'And he always, before...'

'Yes, before. Go on, say it. He was as wild as they come. But he could stand on his own feet in those days. He didn't suffer suicidal moods when the weekends were over and the hangover set in. Did you know he's twice tried to end his life? Do you call that the result of good influence?'

'No!' Dismay darkened her eyes and she put down her untouched drink with unsteady fingers. 'But are you sure that you can blame Rachel for that, any more than—than you can blame me?' she ended in trembling tones.

'I think you know very well my opinion on that matter,' Jordan said grimly, 'which is where you come in.'

She gasped at the hard light of purpose which had narrowed his eyes, and a chill ran through her. None of her fears were imagined; her nebulous dread was crystallised in the reality of Jordan Black's grim expression. He stood up and leaned one arm along the high mantelshelf, and the simple movement seemed to convey his easy power more forcibly than any gesture of clumsy bluster would have done.

He said, 'Rachel would marry Stuart tomorrow, crippled or not, if he'd let her.'

A strange weakness made Gerda limp. The thought of Stuart marrying anyone seemed so alien it stunned her, until she could consider the idea and wonder why it seemed to alien. Why should Stuart *not* marry?

There were many perfectly happy marriages between disabled couples; marriages which frequently held more tight a bond of love because of disabilities fought and overcome than many a union between more fortunate mates. But Rachel . . .

Gerda shook her head, not realising she did so. She knew little of Rachel, but the little she did know failed to convince her that Rachel possessed the stability and the qualities necessary to make a success of a marriage against which the odds were heavily weighted. She was too young, too wild, too impulsive, and in temperament she was too dangerously like Stuart himself.

She looked up almost fearfully into Jordan's dark face. 'You would interfere? Even if they love each other?'

'Interfere?' he almost spat. 'I most certainly would. I'll prevent such a marriage if it's the last thing I do. It's the worst thing that could happen.'

'But are you sure it will happen?'

'Yes. Stuart has retained enough shreds of sense to refuse—so far. But one of these days he's going to say "To hell" and then regret it—as she will.'

'How can you be so certain they'll regret it?'

'Oh, for God's sake! She's only a kid. A spoilt kid who's got this crazy melodramatic notion of taking his life over, making him dependent on her. Use your imagination—if you've got any,' he said scornfully. 'Stuart has to face up to reality. He'll never do that while a crazy neurotic girl persuades him they can shut out the real world and live in a never-never land. According to Rachel *we* are the spiritual cripples, the physical envelope doesn't matter. It's crazy. It's unhealthy. And it's got to stop.'

'Aren't you being unreasonably harsh?' she exclaimed. 'How do you know it's so crazy? How can reality be the same to Stuart as it is to you? He needs someone to help him to adjust. It *is* a different world for him, and how do you know Rachel isn't the only one who's realised it? You can't take her away from him. It would be cruel if he——'

'You're very concerned over his welfare, all of a sudden. I'm delighted at this change of heart. It's going to make it all so much easier.'

'Easier? What do you mean?' she whispered.

He smiled and straightened, to walk to the side of her chair and look down on her upturned face. 'This weekend has been something of an experiment. I think it's been successful.'

He paused, watching her, almost as though he saw beneath the tense composure she strove to maintain to the vulnerability of her to his power. He went on deliberately: 'I wanted to see if Stuart was still attracted to you. I've watched him today, pretty closely, and I think he is. Of course it could be a mere flare of interest in an old face new on the scene, but I don't think it is. My brother went overboard for you three years ago—to his cost—and I don't think he's forgotten. Do you?'

She spread her hands, helpless to scream the denial she longed to fling at him and afraid of the truth he was baring with every word. She remembered Stuart demanding her kiss, trying to invoke her response. She felt the web tightening about her and saw no way of escape....

'And so, my dear Gerda,' the remorseless voice went on, 'you are going to atone for your sins.'

'Atone!' she choked. 'What is this?'

'*You* are going to replace Rachel. You said yourself that Stuart needs someone. So why not you?'

'But—but I can't!' she cried. 'How can I? I——'

'You're a free woman now. It's the ideal solution.'

'No!' She put out one hand, trying to silence him,

and knew she would find no mercy in response to the mute plea.

'Yes.' His hard gaze did not waver. 'If what I suspect is true you married one man out of pity, so why not my brother?'

'You mean ... you mean I should *marry* Stuart?'

'I mean exactly that.'

Her hand fluttered to her throat. 'But I'm not in love with him! He's not in——'

He brushed her trembling protests aside with a curt gesture. 'Love!' There was scorn in his eyes. 'What does love matter in a case like this?'

She shrank back. 'You must be mad!'

'No, my dear Gerda. For my sins I'm many things, but madness isn't one of them.'

He watched her for a moment, then he said abruptly, 'Why don't you admit it? You married Blaise Manston for two reasons. Because you were sorry for him, and because he offered you a way out of the unholy mess you'd made of your affair with Stuart.'

'No! No, that's not true.'

'It's not far off it.'

Suddenly she could not stay still. Hardly knowing what she did or said, she sprang up and went blindly to the window. The skies were silvery dark with midsummer's late dusk and there was still a faint flush low in the west although the day was almost over. A moth fluttered against the pane, and it seemed to symbolise the vain tremors of her own despair. She said in a low voice, 'How can you suggest such a—a cold-blooded arrangement? Just because you're afraid Stuart will make a marriage of which you disapprove. It's the most heartless——'

'Heartless is an ironic accusation from *your* lips,' he said coldly, 'and love an even emptier protest. Tell me,' his mouth curled, 'what is this love you mouth so piously? This love which is so vital to you?'

'You wouldn't listen if I tried to,' she said brokenly, 'and if you did you wouldn't understand.'

'How true.' His silent footfalls fell behind her and she froze as she sensed him at her shoulder. 'Like most of your sex you refuse to face the truth about so-called love. You speak of trust and understanding and unselfishness when the real motive is self-love. Women cry for love and then cry when it hurts them. Because they seek to possess, for self, while they delude themselves they're giving.'

'You're inhuman,' she whispered.

'No, I face facts, and I don't allow sentiment to blind me to what people are.'

His hands closed on her shoulders and his breath stirred her hair. 'This is the great fallacy with which women delude themselves, my dear little hypocrite. It's all misty eyes and honeyed promises of eternal devotion. Faith. Why don't they admit it? That it's all self. The desire to possess. To say: you're mine?'

He tightened his grip and when she moved her head frantically he laughed softly and raked her throat with his mouth. 'That's all it is. Wanting and taking, but pretending it's giving.'

She gave a small cry and twisted free. 'I loathe you,' she choked. 'You're the most callous man I've ever known. You——'

'You'd better be thankful you're not marrying me, then.'

'Marry you!' The words racked her throat. 'Never. And you can't make me marry anyone.'

'No, I can't *make* you.'

Something in his tone made her spin to face him. 'No, it's too preposterous.'

'Is it?' He lounged back idly against the desk. 'I hold two very good cards.'

'Two? I don't know what—— Oh no!' Horror overwhelmed her as she began to suspect his meaning. 'You mean, if I go along with this idea ... this impossible thing ... if I agree, you'll sign the contract?'

'Something like that. Providing, of course, that Stuart wants it that way.'

'It's monstrous!' she gasped. 'It's blackmail!'

'Moral blackmail, my dear Gerda. A fitting conclusion, I think.'

'It's immoral!'

He shrugged, unmoved by her deathly pallor. 'I think you owe it to Stuart.'

She shook her head, as though she could dismiss the nightmare her life had become. Through a haze she stared at the implacable features. 'I—I believe you mean it.'

'I'm not given to saying things I don't mean. You should know me better by now.'

'I don't think I'll ever know you or understand how you could hate so intensely. I——' Her voice faltered and she felt as chill as ice. 'You're not doing this for Stuart. You're trying to satisfy some twisted motive of your own. But why?'

His mouth parted. 'Don't be emotional. The choice is yours. Think it over. Only'—he straightened and his tallness was frightening—'remember this. I can afford to wait. Charingfolds can't.'

She stared wordlessly at him and tried to force her limbs to obey her command. It seemed a long way to the door, and she was hardly conscious of him overtaking her and opening the door with courtesy that seemed a mockery. As she passed him his words echoed over and over again in her brain, only now registering

77

their complete message. She stopped, a prey to a wave of fresh fear.

'You said . . . what did you mean by a—a second card?' she faltered.

He gave a slight smile and stood back.

'That one can wait.'

CHAPTER IV

THE flat held an empty, reproachful air when Gerda got back just after ten the next morning. She dropped her case on a chair and stood in the middle of the room wondering what she should do first. She should telephone Mrs Sanders or the hospital to see what news there was of Howard, and she should get along to the office without any delay.

Oh God, what was she going to do?

In the silence of the flat everything became frighteningly real. During the journey back a numbed apathy had held her emotions dormant, her brain sheering away from the impossible demand Jordan had made the previous evening. He couldn't be serious; she couldn't marry Stuart. It would never work out.

Strangely, Jordan had made no reference to it as he drove back swiftly from Green Rigg. In fact, he had said little to her, apart from the merest formalities. She might have been driving with a stranger or the most casual of acquaintances, and in a paradoxical way he himself had precluded any contemplation of what had happened. It was as though he had dismissed the matter. But she knew instinctively that he was waiting, that the first move had been made and the second one would come when *he* was ready to make it....

When they had reached Grafton Mansions he hadn't got out of the car, pleading lateness for an appointment in the city. He had reached over to open the car door for her, passed her weekend case out to her, given slight smile that had said everything, and said aloud,

79

'See you anon.'

What was she going to do?

The subconscious hope that Howard might have made a miraculous recovery and that somehow the responsibility of the contract would have been lifted from her shoulders was well withered by the end of that miserable Monday.

Howard's condition was still causing a great deal of concern. There was no immediate prospect of his discharge from hospital and he had been warned that a long period of convalescence would be essential when the specialist finally decided to let him leave his sickbed.

'I don't see him being fit enough to come back here in much under a couple of months,' Merrick opined over the afternoon cup of tea in the office, 'but I wish to God he was here today.'

He picked up the memo which had just landed on his desk and scanned it, frowning, then tossed it back into the tray. 'The trouble with Howard is that he kept too much in his head.'

Gerda sighed. 'He used to say he didn't need anything on paper except figures and signatures—and a handshake was best of all.'

Merrick grunted. 'It's all very well playing God if you're immortal. How are we to know what he had in mind? These half-year sheets ... and the deficit on the Sangler exchange,' he groaned. 'What the hell was he going to do about that?'

'He was going to juggle. If we weathered the fall at the end of October we were home and next spring would pay off the gamble.'

Merrick's mouth twisted. 'And if we landed the Van-Lorn contract.'

She was silent, hopeless, then Merrick leaned back

and stretched. 'Of course if we net Wentfords our troubles are over. But I'd be content just to see Howard walk in that door....'

Wouldn't they all? she thought miserably. Something her father had once said came back into her memory. It was fatal for a firm to place too great a dependence on one man. And that was the trouble with Charingfolds. Howard *was* Charingfolds. He inspired confidence, he had an unerring flair for making the right move at the right time, and but for this illness, and the unforeseen snag of Van-Lorn going down to Wentfords, all might have worked out as he planned.

He looked at her so hopefully that evening when she went to visit him that her heart ached and all her previously rehearsed story fled from her mind. She couldn't tell him she'd spent the weekend at Black's home, or even that she'd seen Black during the weekend and discussed the contract; now she found she couldn't even tell him she'd been in touch with Black and the negotiations were hopeful.

She kissed him and gave a sad little shake of her head. 'I'm sorry. I was hoping there would be some news today, but there isn't—not just yet.'

Howard made a brave effort to hide his disappointment. He touched her hand. 'Don't look so worried, my dear. I know you're doing your best and I think you're being wonderful, so try not to fret.' He smiled. 'I'm not.'

But she knew he was, in spite of his determined cheerfulness as she sat and talked to him, and her heart was heavy when she got back to the flat and listlessly caught up with her personal chores.

By the time she climbed into bed, weary but knowing sleep would not be easily won, she believed she had reached the nadir of despair. Why should so many people's lives and happiness be at the mercy of Jordan Black? Why should he be able to drop the stone in the pool of life and watch the ripples spread to affect not only herself and Howard Durrel, but all the unknown lives which would ultimately be affected by his action? And why did she have to be the cardinal point?

She stared into the darkness and found no answer except the overwhelming agony of a heart divided. If only there were solace in telling herself over and over again how much she hated Jordan Black. Hatred: *too akin to love.* ... His words. Her hatred; her ...

She buried her face in the pillow and then stiffened as the phone shrilled in the midnight stillness.

Instantly the fears began to race. Who? At midnight?

Jordan?

She started up, groping for the lamp switch, despising herself for flying to his name, then experienced the tremor of remorse. Howard! Oh no! Not that!

She thrust her arm into her wrap and stumbled into the lounge, the folds of the wrap trailing behind her. She snatched at the phone, fearing the ringing would stop before she ... and gasped her number.

'Hello, Gerda. Did I wake you up?'

The sense of relief when she recognised Stuart's voice brought a weakness near fainting point. For a moment she couldn't respond, and he said sharply: 'Are you there, Gerda? Are you all right?'

'Yes. Just a moment.' She gathered the wrap about her and sank down on the telephone stool. 'I—I wasn't expecting you—anyone—and I thought it was bad news—Howard Durrel. He's ill.'

'I'm sorry. I must have got you out of bed as well.' Stuart sounded contrite. There was a heavy sigh at the other end of the line. 'I couldn't sleep, and I was think-

82

ing about you, so I decided to ring you up.'

'Oh.' She was relaxing, reaching the point of pleasure after relief that it wasn't ... 'Actually, I wasn't asleep either. I'd just turned in.'

'Are you too tired to talk to me?'

'No, not really.'

'I often ring Rachel up during the night and we talk for hours. It's fun to talk over the phone when everyone else is asleep and you know that no one is going to interrupt. But I wanted to talk to you.'

He paused, as though expecting her to make some comment, then went on: 'It was strange meeting you again. Not a bit like I expected.'

'What did you expect?' she asked idly.

'I dunno. Did you enjoy the weekend?'

'Yes,' she lied.

'Will you come for another one very soon?'

'I—I—— Yes, if you want me to,' she said after a hesitation, 'if——'

'If Jordan's there?' he cut in rather sharply, then, with a suggestion of a chuckle, 'Or if Jordan's *not* there?'

'Isn't he always home at weekends?' she said carefully.

'Jordan? Good heavens, no! He hates the sight of the gang. Gerda?'

'Yes.'

'How long have you been back in Jordan's orbit?'

The note of suspicion was unmistakable. She said slowly: 'I would hardly say I was back. Last week was the first time I'd seen him for three years. Didn't he tell you?'

'He told me on Friday night that he'd been wining and dining with my ex-love.'

Ex-love. Stuart's or Jordan's words? 'There was only

the one occasion,' she said, 'and it was business.'

There was a pause. 'That contract? It's taking a hell of a time to settle, isn't it?'

She closed her eyes. *Who* was taking the hell of a time?

Stuart said, 'What's he playing at?'

'I don't know. Is he?'

'He is. Jordan never does anything without a reason.'

Who should know better than his own brother? she thought wearily, and wondered if Stuart knew. After a moment of reflection she decided it was unlikely that he did. They had left early that morning after a brief goodbye to Stuart who had been too sleepy-eyed to do anything but murmur a drowsy response.

'Gerda ...?'

'Mm?' She huddled the receiver closer and eased her cramped foot.

'I've often wondered ... it never occurred to me until a long time afterwards ...'

'What?'

'Was there anything between you and Jordan?'

He must have heard her slight gasp. He said sharply: 'There was! I don't know why I was so blind. All that time ago it was my dear brother and I never guessed. And he never breathed a word. Well, of all the——' Suddenly Stuart was laughing, unbelievably ironic laughter.

It stilled into silence, a silence that made him say abruptly: 'Are you still there?'

'Yes,' she forced the words from a tight throat, 'but you're mistaken. Jordan never had time for me or even thought of——'

'Darling!' he was chuckling again, 'you needn't be afraid, not now. Did you know we used to swap girls sometimes? If we weren't serious about them. But then

84

Jordan was never serious about girls.'

This was no surprise, but the ice stabbed in her heart.

'Except Diane, of course.'

Diane!

'Is—is she his fiancée?'

'Diane? Good heavens, no. She'd like to nail him, I guess, but she'll be lucky if she manages it.'

'Oh,' was all Gerda could manage. 'I—I didn't know.'

'Of course, I forget. You've been off the scene so long. Diane's been pretty steady on it for about a year now.' A malicious note entered Stuart's tone. 'She's quite a honey—if you go for the generous Italian-armful type.'

'Is she Italian?'

'No. Pure home-grown. But I guess she could take a lesson from your expertise in bringing a man up to scratch.'

The dark shadows in the room seemed to gather closer about her. She shivered. The ice was deadening the pain and her heart felt like lead. The voice against her ear said: 'No comment?'

'No comment,' she said dully.

'I'm disappointed.'

'Are you? Stuart, it's awfully late and I'm frozen. Do you mind if——?'

'Cold, darling? A lovely warm night like this? You must be——'

'Yes, I know, but I have a job to go to tomorrow. Couldn't you manage to go to sleep now?'

'I'll try. Are you coming down again soon?'

'If you like,' she said wearily.

'You do sound bushed, my love. I'll let you go—till tomorrow. Sleep well.'

That was the beginning of the midnight phone

assignations with Stuart. It seemed to give him pleasure to talk and reminisce, often about friends of his who were only names to Gerda, about Leon, Rachel, and about Jordan.

She hadn't the heart to curtail the calls, even though the strain was taking its toll by mid-week. If it helped Stuart to face his lonely crippled nights it did not matter so much that it was the reverse for Gerda as she lay sleepless into the early hours of the morning. Nor could she refuse Stuart's invitation to spend the coming weekend at Green Rigg. There was a small solace in the fact that the invitation seemed unprompted by Jordan, who, as far as she could gather, was unlikely to be at home, and unless Stuart had become a more expert dissembler than she believed him to be he was genuinely unaware of his brother's grim plan for Gerda. What would Stuart say if he knew? she wondered. Stuart had his faults, but they included neither vindictiveness nor guile. Emotion or fear could trick him into evasion—a very human failing—but never deliberate chicanery.

Perhaps Jordan's cruel efforts might be proved unnecessary, she thought bitterly, for the first time wondering if her own unhappiness and compassion might yet lead her into sacrificing her own desires. Why fight the dark fates? It seemed they had long planned to destroy any hopes of future happiness and worked their dark pattern through those she most loved. First her beloved parents, then Blaise, finally even Stuart, whom she had loved in her way but not in the way he had desired, and Howard, to whom she owed loyalty as well as affection. And above them all loomed the dark lodestar of Jordan Black. Why should one man hold the power to destroy her—or give her heaven?

Looking back on the past four years, could she have

86

acted differently? Could she have taken any alternative course? Why, even now, could she not turn her back on it all and run? Away, anywhere, where she knew no one and where she could try to forget?

By the Thursday there was a slight improvement in Howard's condition. For the first time he was allowed up for a short while, and Merrick was overjoyed.

'We'll have him back at the helm in no time,' he enthused.

Gerda knew differently. She, who had visited him most frequently, knew that the doctor's warnings were not idle ones. Stress could prove dangerous now after the weakening of the heart condition and it would be a long time before Howard was fit to resume his former pace—if ever, she thought in the darker moments. But she kept these fears to herself. The only thing they could do was to cheer him as much as they were able and try to keep his worries at bay.

At times she had wild notions of appealing to Jordan, pleading with him to relent, no matter how humbled she must be, but bitterness stayed her hand when she would have reached for the phone, bitterness and the fear of failure. In these moments fierce resentment of Merrick possessed her. He seemed to be doing so little, content to mark time and keep things ticking over, and settling into a fatalistic mood of what's to be will be. He wasn't a worrier, she thought. Which was why he would never reach Howard's stature.

Strangely enough, she felt a strange sense of loss when the now familiar summons did not shrill late on the Thursday evening. She knew Stuart would not telephone later than midnight and decided the novelty of those oddly intimate little exchanges had worn off. More probable was that he thought it unnecessary now the weekend was so near, so that when the phone rang just after eleven as she was settling down to sleep on the Friday night she experienced a start of surprise.

'I'm going to bring you a supply of sleeping pills, my lad,' she grumbled not unkindly as she raised the receiver to her ear.

'I never need them,' said Jordan.

She gasped, and he said: 'Who did you think it was?'

'Stuart,' she said, and waited.

'I gather he's been in touch with you,' Jordan went on without preamble, 'and you're coming down tomorrow.'

'Yes.'

'Good. I didn't expect to be free, but I'll pick you up at midday.'

'You don't need to bother. It's all arranged,' she said stiffly. 'I'm coming down by train and Leon is going to meet me.'

'I'll take you. It's lousy travelling by train at weekends once the holiday season gets under way.'

'I don't mind that. It's——'

'It's too late too argue. I'll pick you up noon sharp and we'll have lunch on the way down. So long.'

He rang off before she could make any further objection, leaving her staring at the receiver. His brusqueness stirred anger in her and she was still nettled when he arrived and lounged coolly into her flat.

'Smoke?'

'No, thanks.' A perverseness made her slow her last-minute preparations for leaving, and even hover unnecessarily in the kitchenette although she had already checked that she had left everything in order.

'Left the gas on?' From the doorway he watched her with sardonic eyes.

'No.' She brushed past him and went into the bed-

88

room to collect her jacket. Holding it over her arm and carrying her case, she stood in the hall, pointedly waiting.

'You've left a transom open.' With unflurried movements he attended the one thing she had been about to do at the moment of his arrival. He glanced round the immaculate flat, then at her. 'You look displeased. Is the prospect of being my sister-in-law still unappealing?'

'That's not funny,' she said through tight lips. 'I thought I'd made my feelings perfectly clear about that prospect. Shall we go?'

'In a moment.' Almost dispassionately he considered the proud defiant eyes that steadfastly refused to waver under his stare. 'I'm well aware that you loathe me pretty thoroughly, that you consider me callous and ruthless. But I would remind you of two things, Gerda. One of them seems to matter very much to you. I'm not sure why Charingfolds and this contract are so important to you. My employees are reasonably loyal to me, but I doubt if they'd lose much sleep on my account. I can only conclude there is a strong personal involvement in your relationship with Howard Durrel, who stands to lose most if the contract fails to materialise. *Are* you having an affair with him?'

'It has nothing to do with you if I am.'

'No, but it would explain a great deal.'

'Is there anything to explain?' she asked coldly. 'Why don't you admit that your terms are perfectly clear, and perfectly crude?'

'No, because the moral aspect is neither clear nor crude.'

'Moral is the last description I'd apply to your proposition!' she flashed.

'You are thinking only of your point of view, the

thing that matters to you.' He shifted his weight and glanced at his watch. 'I'm thinking of my brother. He matters a great deal to me.'

'I wonder if anyone or anything matters to you.' She shifted her case to her other hand, and with a muttered aside he stepped forward and took it from her. She resisted, then wearily released her grasp, afraid of the contact of his warm hand against her own chill fingers. She looked away. 'What is it you want to say?'

'That you have a moral responsibility towards my brother, and don't you ever forget it.'

'Will you ever let me?' she returned.

'Not if I can help it,' he said grimly, then put a hand on her arm as she made to move away. 'There's one more thing ...!'

She stood silent, refusing to look at him, wanting only to bring the conversation to an end before he imprinted any more memories of his presence on her only haven, her home.

'Don't make my brother care again, and then destroy him. If you do ...' his mouth hardened and the hand on her arm fell away, 'I swear you'll regret it.'

Abruptly he swung the door open and waited till she had preceded him. He checked that the door was securely closed and without speaking accompanied her from the building. As they emerged the sun was hot, reflecting a blinding powdery glare from the white forecourt, but Gerda felt only a dull inward chill as she walked to the green Mercedes.

*   •   •   ➤

Jordan left her immediately they arrived at Green Rigg and it was not till some time later that she discovered he had returned to the city.

'I hope he comes down tomorrow,' Stuart remarked. 'I've got a little surprise for him.'

She murmured a response, not really hearing the second part of Stuart's remark. Why had Jordan insisted on bringing her down? Had he made a not inconsiderable journey that morning merely to issue the warning that still struck a chill sense of unease whenever she thought of it?

Aware that Stuart was waiting for her to reply, she shrugged and saw a frown replace the meaning light in his eyes.

'What's going on, Gerda?'

'What? Nothing's going on. What could be going on?' She instilled a careless note into the question.

'That's what I'm asking you, darling.' Stuart swivelled to within reach of a big bowl of fruit and selected a peach, studying it critically. He held it out to her and took one for himself. 'You have a guilty look about something.'

She nearly dropped the peach. She recovered and bit into the soft luscious fruit before she replied: 'I'm worried. I—I was thinking about Howard, and—various other things,' she evaded.

Stuart looked steadily at her and weighed the peach in his hand. 'I wonder. I have become expert at reading expressions—and what they hide.' He picked up a small silver fruit knife and neatly extracted the stone. 'I've had lots of time and lots of opportunity for practice. Now, take Jordan, for instance ...'

He paused, and she knew she had failed to conceal an instinctive tensing. 'Jordan was supposed to be meeting a very important man this weekend. This very important bod was stopping over in London en route from the States to Brussels and Munich. Because of this VIB,' Stuart continued in measured tones, 'Jordan stood up Diane after promising her a riotous weekend at some crony's place up the Thames. Poor little Diane was very upset. She even tried to weep a tiny tear, but broke a claw peeling the onion. Or so——'

'Stuart! You heartless wretch. You sound like a girl's worst friend.' Gerda laughed uneasily, hoping to divert him from the subject of his brother. 'You should be ashamed of yourself.'

'I was using Rachel's kindly little surmise of Diane's reaction,' he said blandly. 'Those two are noble friends, quite devoted to each other. I'm sure they're going to love you as well.'

'No doubt,' she said dryly. 'You're dribbling juice on your shirt.'

'No matter.' Stuart swallowed the last morsel of peach. 'But in view of all this, why should Jordan take up a whole precious morning to collect and deliver you?'

'How should I know? I told him last night he needn't bother.'

'Aha! I knew there was something. So you were with him last night.' A flash of malicious triumph crossed Stuart's face. 'I knew he was two-timing me—trying to kid me you just dropped back out of the blue, then dropping you back in my lap. Why? What's going on?'

'You're imagining things.'

'I'm not. I knew it last weekend, and I'm positive now.' Stuart's expression had changed from semi-serious banter to sharp suspicion. 'Listen, Gerda. For nearly three years you might not have existed as far as Jordan was concerned. Then suddenly you're here, thrust at me, and you look scared stiff of your own shadow one minute and as guilty as hell the next. While Big Brother looks as calculating as old Nick himself.'

Stuart propelled his chair along until he was at the other side of her chair. The silent movement behind was strangely disturbing and she rubbed her fingers nervously on a handkerchief. 'You know already, Stuart. It's the truth. I never saw Jordan until a couple of weeks ago.'

Stuart did not seem to be listening. Suddenly his mouth compressed. He gave her a sharp look. 'You never told him, did you?'

'No,' she looked down, 'I never told him.'

'Thank God for that—there'd have been hell to pay. I think we kept it dark from him, but knowing Jordan ...' Stuart passed a thin hand over his brow. 'Those days after the smash were very hazy. When I think back to them I can't recall everything that happened. The only thing I remembered clearly was that nobody had to know, except us.'

She sighed. 'Forget it. Nobody's likely to know now, except us,' she said quietly.

Stuart was silent, his face softened with reflection. At last he said wryly: 'We weren't very kind to you, were we?'

Abruptly she stood up and walked across to where a picture was propped on top of a cabinet. 'Is this one of yours?'

'Yeah. It's lousy.'

'I don't think so.' She studied the apparently formal, almost insipid depiction of sand dunes deserted at sunset. The sea had a red-hazed, oily calm and there was a sense of all life departed from the scene. 'Did you have to put the tide of litter in—after the trippers went home? It's rather——' She stopped, a tremor of horror running through her as the concealed forms within the picture were revealed. 'When did you do this?' she exclaimed. 'It—it's macabre!'

'You've discerned my skulls?' There was satisfaction in Stuart's expression, as though her betrayal of shock pleased him. 'That was during my period of Dali influence. Before I discovered how little talent I had for painting. But it makes a talking point.'

'I think you enjoy shocking people.' She turned away from the disturbing picture.

'It's one of the few things left I can enjoy,' he rejoined dryly. 'A drink?'

'Yes, please.'

He mixed two drinks, two long ones, clinking ice into the chunky glasses and adding a scarlet crystal swizzle-stick to Gerda's. 'Well, come and get it,' he ordered, 'and say thank you in the proper way.'

'You mean pay for it,' she returned steadily, eyeing the hand that had imprisoned her wrist.

'Isn't that part of the plan?' He dropped her hand and smiled cynically. 'I'm not totally stupid, you know.'

'I never thought you were.' She retreated to an armchair and sank into it. 'Where are Rachel and Leon?'

'Gone to Eastbourne.'

'Aren't you jealous? In case they get ideas about each other?' she amended hastily, afraid lest he should think she meant their ability to be independent.

'Not in the least. Rachel is mine.'

She sipped at her drink, conscious of strain and wondering how long she could maintain composure against Stuart's probing. Cruel as Jordan might be, she had to admit that his concern for his young brother was justified. The previous weekend she had believed him to be unjustified in his assertions about Stuart's attitude towards life; now she knew differently. His former recklessness had been frustrated by disability and had taken the form of despotism. It was understandable, forgivable, but the morbid streak was disturbing. For once she found herself in agreement with Jordan; it was unhealthy.

'So we come back to you,' Stuart said softly. 'Have you really discovered after all this time that I mean something to you? Or are you the thin end of the wedge?'

She stared, and he laughed. 'Stop pretending, darling. Why not admit that you're the start of the softening-up process?'

A dreadful conviction was born in her that he knew and was taking a malicious pleasure in taunting her with his knowledge. She stared at his cynical young face and wondered how to counter the impossible situation between the two brothers.

But Stuart did not bother waiting for her answer. He said bitterly, 'It's so obvious it shrieks. Jordan is hoping you'll succeed where he has failed.'

'But how has he failed?' she exclaimed.

'Jordan is a born manager of other people's lives. He's always been the same. His father's son. He's hard and he's bigoted, and he holds the purse-strings, blast him.' Abruptly Stuart wheeled about and stopped by the window, staring out at the stillness of green. His profile was set and sharply edged with anger.

'Why the hell do I have to be dependent on him? Sometimes I wish I'd never been born,' he burst out. 'If my mother hadn't been a soft sentimental fool I wouldn't have been. Oh, for God's sake go away and leave me. I don't want you. I don't want anybody!'

The suddenness of his outburst shocked her. For a moment she stood aghast, then the tragic outline of the dark head above the back of the wheelchair evoked a flood of pity and she forgot her own fears and despair.

She ran to him and knelt by his side.

'Stuart...' she put out a tentative hand, 'what is all this? Can't you tell me? You—you can't mean all these things. I'm sure Jordan—— Are you sure——?' She stopped helplessly, searching the dark moody features with worried eyes.

'It is true,' he said sombrely, 'but you don't want to hear it all.'

'If it helps you to talk, then tell me. If not,' she hesitated, 'I'll go away.'

'No,' he clutched at her hand and held it tight, 'don't go away again. It's just that—— Oh, it never seemed to matter before—before all this happened. Jordan and I got along all right. We didn't have to see enough of each other to get on each other's nerves, and I didn't have to be dependent on him. You see... light me a ciggy, darling, please,' he interjected, obviously making an effort to recover from his outburst, and avoided her gaze as she did so. 'You see, my parents split up when Jordan was a kid—I won't tell you all the sordid details except that my father was a brute and my mother is sweet but hopelessly ineffectual, and that helps to explain the differences between Jordan and me. After she ran away my father had a free hand in Jordan's upbringing. He sent him to one of these ghastly schools where you get up in the middle of the night and break the ice to wash, and cover a couple of assault courses to get up an appetite for breakfast—if you survive till breakfast, that is. But to get back to the parents; they had a reconciliation when Jordan was fourteen, of which I was the result, and which accounts for the generation gap between us. We're poles apart, never mind generations, and I suppose I can count myself lucky that Father began to soften in his dotage or I'd have suffered the same treatment.'

'You must have been very young when your father died,' she said sympathetically.

'He died the day after my tenth birthday. I'll always remember it because I'd kicked up a stink because he wouldn't give me a gun. Then he relented the next day and said he would. That was at breakfast. By night...' Stuart shrugged and went on: 'Jordan took over the business. Straight away. My father's shoes were exactly the right size for him, and he was more than tough enough to wear them.'

'Someone had to take over,' she said gently. 'There wasn't anyone else but Jordan.'

Stuart's mouth remained obstinate, and she felt obliged to point out the obvious, despite her antipathy towards Jordan. 'You might have found everything very difficult now, but for Jordan. Be fair. He's tried to smooth life for you. He's done everything humanly possible.'

'Oh yes, I'll admit it. But why doesn't he let me get on with it my own way?' Stuart cried. 'But no. He comes down here and disapproves of my friends. He's damned rude to Rachel. He reads the riot act because we game. He screams at the drink bill. What else does he expect me to do? Drinking and gaming are about the only amusements I have left.'

Gerda was silent. There was little she could say. The opposing brothers were both right—and both wrong. But there wasn't any answer she could see, except...

'So I'm waiting, Gerda.' He looked up at her and gave a twisted smile.

'For it all to work out magically?' she said with a weary gesture.

'No. I'm waiting for you to begin your persuasive pep talk.'

'Pep talk?' She stared. 'What do you mean?'

97

'Now don't go all innocent. Jordan has had the bright idea of bringing you back, in the hope you'll resuscitate the old spark. That you'll be able to talk me into letting the sawbones experiment. Isn't that true?'

He was so near the truth she was aghast, and for a moment the temptation to tell him the actual facts was very strong. Then she reluctantly put it away from her. Whatever happened she could not be the means of inciting further acrimony between the brothers. Stuart was so utterly mistaken in his suspicion. Perhaps Jordan had been overbearing—it was not difficult to understand how his patience had been tried to the limit—but he had Stuart's interest at heart. So much that he was prepared to inflict heartbreak on herself and others in order to further that interest. Her heart was heavy as she grasped at the only answer she could make. She shook her head.

'No, Stuart. For once you've misjudged him. He never said a word about your going for an operation, or refusing it, or anything. I swear it.'

'He will.'

She shook her head again, unable to deny his assurance with any certainty.

'Well, if he does, I don't want to hear about it, and not from you, Gerda. It's my life and no one's going to tell me what I have to do or haven't to do. Do you understand?'

She nodded miserably and for a little while there was a silence. Then he wheeled slowly to the fitted desk unit along one wall and took out a bottle of tablets. She watched him swallow two with a drink of water and asked: 'What are those?' more to break the uncomfortable silence than because she was curious.

He gestured carelessly. 'When the world looks black they help to lighten it to grey. Gerda...?'

'Yes.' She turned, and felt a pang as she saw the melancholy in his dark eyes. Obeying the hand he stretched out towards her, she went to his side and tried to smile. 'Cheer up, Stuart, or they'll blame me when they get back and see you like this.'

'They know me better than you do, darling. Are you sure that Jordan isn't using you as a lever?'

'To force you to change your mind? No, Stuart. I didn't know until you told me yourself.'

Something in her steady gaze must have convinced him, for he nodded slowly and a trace of his cynicism flashed. 'But you agree with him, don't you?'

'Yes, and I can't promise not to try to persuade you to think it over,' she said slowly.

He held her gaze for a long moment as though he was seeking to read truth in her eyes, then he said intently: 'Does it matter to you what becomes of me?'

'Of course it matters! You have most of your life in front of you. You mustn't give up hope, and you mustn't waste your life.'

'Just like that! You really believe there's a miracle round the corner, don't you?'

'No, not a miracle,' she said quietly, 'but opportunity and hope.'

He sighed deeply and touched her hand. 'Gerda, don't go out of my life again. Promise?'

CHAPTER V

RACHEL and Leon returned a little while later, loaded with parcels, from their trip into Eastbourne.

Leon's greeting to Gerda was friendly enough, but Rachel's was little short of surly and she made no effort to conceal her resentment of Gerda's presence. A vivid little figure in a rainbow-patterned tunic over jade green trousers, she monopolised the conversation at dinner as though Gerda was not present. However, Stuart had regained a brighter mood, so Gerda fought down her natural reaction to take refuge in frigid silence and tried not to show her hurt when they gathered in Stuart's apartment after dinner to play the batch of new records Rachel had bought.

Leon turned out some of the lights and with the start of the music Rachel's artificial gaiety left her. For a long time she stayed silent, lying flat on a divan with her hands pillowed under her head and staring unwinkingly at the ceiling. When the record ended she refused to be drawn into a discussion of it, but when Leon put on the theme music from a currently popular film she suddenly came to life. With slow, studied movements she carried the scarlet footstool over to Stuart and set it down close to his side, where she sat down and began quite blatantly to caress him, almost as though she defied onlookers to watch.

Stuart himself neither encouraged nor repulsed her, his slight smile inscrutable and his shadowed eyes holding a faraway expression, almost as though he was unaware of the slender arm curved about his neck and the small hand that explored his face with slow, sensuous caresses. Finally she curled her feet up under her and laid her head in his lap, her long hair tumbling like black silk over his knees. He did look down at her then and began to stroke her hair, running his fingers through it and shaping it into thick, ordered spirals where it lay.

Leon seemed unmoved by the careless intimacy, but Gerda found it disturbing. She had never been able to demonstrate affection under strangers' eyes, and to Rachel she must be a stranger. She tried to concentrate on the music and keep her gaze averted, then she heard a stifled gasp and saw Leon laughing.

Stuart was edging his chair back, infinitely slowly, while Rachel hung on to his knees until it was inevitable that she should fall. The stool tipped, and abruptly she tried to save herself. She scrambled up and her face was scarlet with rage.

'Beast! Beast!' she screamed. 'I hate you! I hate you all!'

Openly weeping now, she fled out of the room.

The two men met Gerda's shocked gaze. Leon shrugged, and Stuart grinned heartlessly. 'She'll get over it. She's a creature of moods, our Rachel.'

'But ...' Gerda stood up. 'Shouldn't somebody ...?' She gestured towards the door.

'Good heavens, no. She wouldn't thank you.' Stuart reached over the side of his chair and set the footstool to rights. 'Actually, she thoroughly enjoys it. Aren't you going to take over the soothing of my fevered brow?' He patted the stool invitingly.

'No, I'm not.' Suddenly Gerda felt she couldn't take any more. She had been thankful when she had learned that Jordan would not be back that day, but now she would have welcomed his presence. At least you could predict with reasonable accuracy what to expect from Jordan and so armour yourself accordingly, but there were undercurrents here with Stuart and Rachel that disturbed and almost frightened her. With a murmured excuse she got up and escaped to her room.

The silence of the countryside at night was oppressive and disturbing to Gerda in her present troubled mood. The air was hot and clammy, and she would have welcomed even the familiar sounds of the nocturnal traffic which were a constant lullaby outside her own home. Here there wasn't a whisper and she spent a restless night that seemed endless.

Morning brought clouded skies and a heavy thundery atmosphere that sapped vitality. Gerda looked through the curtains and wondered whether to get up or go back to bed. It wasn't quite seven and there wasn't a sound to suggest that anyone else apart from herself was astir in the house.

She sat on the edge of the bed, and the day ahead seemed to beckon with foreboding. Was that how Stuart and Rachel always behaved? Taunting, loving, quarrelling? It was a strange and stormy relationship to Gerda's eyes. What happiness did it bring them? And how was she herself to fit into it? Whichever way she looked at it she could foresee only unhappiness. Couldn't Jordan see that? Why couldn't she have the courage to defy him? To run before she was drawn any tighter into the web, before ... even if it meant failing Howard. Even if it ...

A tap at the door jerked her back to the present. Before she could move or respond a light voice said: 'Are you awake? It's tea,' and Leon opened the door.

Seeming quite unembarrassed by her somewhat flustered scramble back under the covers, he set the tray down and crossed to the window.

'Shall I draw your curtains—or leave the beastly day shut out?'

'Oh, open them, please. Thank you for bringing the tea. I—I didn't expect it.'

Leon gave his quiet smile. 'I usually do the honours on a Sunday to give Mrs B her Sunday off.'

He seemed inclined to chat and she said idly: 'Why do you all call her Mrs B?'

'Because Bredlingham is a long name and we're all lazy.'

'Oh.' She nibbled one of the biscuits and wondered about Leon. Was he a trained nurse? How did he cope with Stuart's black moods? He seemed an easy-going young man, unflappable, and part of the family rather than an employee. Stuart was fortunate to have him.

She looked up and surprised Leon's glance. He said lightly: 'It isn't as bad as it appears.'

When she continued to stare at him he went on: 'You were worried last night. I couldn't say anything at the time, but I thought I should perhaps mention it now. On surface appearance Stuart treats Rachel very unkindly and she acts like a temperamental little slave. But they understand each other extremely well. More important, each provides the other with a safety valve.'

He paused, then turned to leave, looking back at her when he reached the door and giving that reserved smile of his. 'Don't let it worry you and don't let your concern show. All right?'

It wasn't exactly a note of apology in the final query, more an injunction. To do what? she wondered after he had gone, and as she dressed the conviction grew in her that Leon had been issuing a kind of warning. But why?

She could not completely dismiss the memory as the

day began to take shape, nor could she entirely fathom Leon's meaning. She remembered Jordan's fear of a marriage between his brother and the strange young girl who seemed so devoted to him and wondered if Leon was in their confidence. Were they already planning to defy Jordan's wishes? But if so, what could she do about it? In her heart, did she want to prevent it, even if she had the power to do so, which seemed unlikely in spite of Jordan's dictatorial assertion?

Rachel was surprisingly gay that morning, betraying no sign of the stormy outburst the evening before. They went out into the garden after breakfast and Rachel dragged an old croquet set out of the summer-house.

'Anybody know how to play?' she demanded.

No one did. Stuart said, 'You knock the ball through the hoops—I think.'

'No! Not really!' Rachel hammered at one of the hoops, regardless of the damage she was inflicting on the velvety lawn. The mallet narrowly missed her finger and she swore violently. 'Are you helpless, Leon?' she snapped.

He went to help her and Stuart grinned. 'You look like the Queen of Hearts in that scarlet skirt.'

'As long as it isn't the queen of tarts,' she retorted, measuring out paces to the next hoop. 'I'm doing this for you, you know? You can play from your chair and beat us all.'

'With my flamingo under my arm?'

'Pig!'

'You know you adore me—Pepper!'

Gerda had a distinct sensation of being there yet not there. They played a game of croquet that was as unorthodox as that played in any child's Wonderland, until the clouds gathered more darkly and as the first

104

heavy drops fell a white sports car raced up the drive and skidded to a halt.

A dark girl in a coral shirt and skin-tight cream pants got out and came across the lawn. She said carelessly, 'Hi, there,' and the skies opened.

'You brought this with you, Diane,' Stuart grumbled as they rushed for shelter. 'You know Gerda? Gerda—Diane.'

The dark girl gave Gerda a casual nod and smoothed the raindrops off her hair. 'Where's Jordan?'

'Not here,' said Stuart with a malicious quirk of his brows. 'Did you expect him to be here?'

'When you asked me over—yes. Is he still tied up with this business deal, or whatever it is?'

Stuart grinned. 'There's the deal he's tied up with—sitting over there.'

'Really?' Diane surveyed Gerda with unfriendly eyes. 'Pull the other one for a change.' She accepted a drink and lounged back in a chair, apparently quite at home.

She wasn't beautiful in a classical sense. Her mouth was too full and her eyes rather deep-set, but she was undoubtedly attractive with her vivid colouring and there was a slumbrous quality about her that suggested a dormant fire.

They had almost finished lunch when Jordan walked in. He seemed taken aback when he saw Diane and his glance swivelled to Gerda for a second before returning to Diane. 'I didn't expect to see you here.'

She smiled, perfectly at ease. 'Didn't you know? I'm Stuart's surprise.'

His brows flickered. 'I'm duly surprised. But I can't take you out, honey.'

'No matter.' The curve of her mouth was bold. 'There's tomorrow and all the other tomorrows. Have you eaten, darling?'

'Yes, but I'll have some coffee.'

He watched her as she poured it and took it to him, sitting on the arm of his chair and idly drawing circles in the air with one sandalled foot. She leaned slightly towards him, talking in soft tones that did not reach into the room and allowing the curve of her body to brush against his shoulder.

There was no attempt to disguise the shared looks of intimacy or the smouldering sense in the way they spoke softly while Jordan drank the coffee.

Gerda tried not to watch. So this was Jordan's girl! She knew all the signs and despised herself for suffering the dagger stabs of disillusion. Why should she be such a fool as to imagine Jordan's life to be one of celibacy? Jordan was in the mid-thirties, unmarried. He'd be abnormal if he lived without feminine interest. But Diane ... The girl was so obvious, so voluptuous.... Gerda accepted a cigarette from Leon and made a determined effort to ignore Jordan, but her imagination persisted in filling in those shadowed gaps in his life which Diane shared....

● ■ ●

It poured steadily all the afternoon. Shortly after three Jordan excused himself, pleading pressure of work.

Diane was plainly put out and said so.

But now he was not to be swayed by provocative appeals. He gave her a level look. 'You should know me better by now, honey. I don't arrange weekends with a girl like you and then neglect her. That's why I cancelled our trip.'

'Then why ask me here?' she pouted, following him

106

to the door.

'But *I* didn't.' He touched her cheek and the gesture was agonisingly familiar to Gerda. 'But you don't have to run away. Make yourself at home.'

Almost as though he dismissed Diane, he glanced back and said to no one in particular: 'Will somebody ask Mrs B to bring me a tray of something cold around seven?'

Leon responded, and Jordan went out, presumably to shut himself up in his study with whatever work it was he wanted to attend to.

Diane lingered on until afternoon tea and then departed. No one made any attempt to persuade her to delay, and Gerda wondered for a wild moment if she should also simply get up and go. She went to help Leon who had begun to remove the tea debris and was thankful to escape to the kitchen, even to the mundane business of being the guest who washed up. The rain continued to pour down and there was a hypnotic quality in the relentless beating against the window. It seemed to trap them all and depress their spirits, sapping any effort to repulse the mood of melancholy it engendered.

'This is a typical English Sunday in the country,' Stuart said.

And this was the most uncomfortable weekend she had ever spent, Gerda reflected, trying to console herself with the thought that only a few hours remained of the evening and tomorrow morning she would be back in the comparative normality of her working routine.

The others settled down to watch a film on television. They armed themselves with drinks and smokes and salted nuts and an enormous packet of crisps. The room grew darker and Gerda became increasingly restless. At last she gave up trying to keep her attention on the screen and got up quietly.

No one heeded her going and she let herself out on to the terrace.

The rain had stopped at last, leaving the air clear and fresh, and she strolled slowly along till she came to the path through the garden. She did not want to stay out very long. The closeness had gone out of the air and it was cool enough to induce a shiver. After a few minutes she turned to retrace her steps, intending to return indoors, but when she reached the flat paved walk she felt a strange reluctance to move on.

She rested her hands on the back of the garden seat and faced the root cause of her restlessness. Jordan Black was within the house, and even unseen his presence reached out to her through the barriers of bricks and mortar. Thoughts of Diane invaded her mind, thoughts she would not have admitted to a single soul. They were compounded of dislike, wild unreasoning envy, and pity. Dislike because Diane was brash, self-assured, and she radiated the kind of aura that was instantly antagonistic to other women; envy because she was part of Jordan's life, because he probably loved her as much as his nature would permit him to love any woman, and because she must know what it was like to experience his tenderness and his passion. Strangely enough, Gerda could summon pity because she knew it was inevitable that Diane would suffer at his hands sooner or later. For any woman who was foolish enough to love Jordan Black was doomed to get hurt.

Unless Diane was wise enough not to love him. Maybe she was clever enough and hard enough to take and give without letting her heart stand the cost. Maybe she merely enjoyed the purely superficial side of the affair, being escorted and spoiled, for Jordan would be generous in material things, of this Gerda was certain, and the voluptuous satisfaction of being made love to, for in this also Jordan would undoubtedly prove no less generous than expert.

She shivered, turning sharply as though she could escape her thoughts, and found him facing her.

She gasped and took an involuntary step back. 'I—I didn't hear you!'

'You were miles away from hearing anything.' He rested his hands on the back of the seat, exactly as she had done, and looked down at them. 'You seemed to be trying to reach some decision. Were you?'

'Not especially.'

He turned his head. 'Has it been a disappointing weekend?'

'No, it—it's been a very wet one,' she said with an attempt at lightness.

'True.' He straightened, and surprised the tremor that ran through her as she instinctively tensed before his movement. 'What's the matter? Are you cold?'

'No—yes—a little. I think——'

'Make your mind up. Or shall I do it for you?' He put his arm round her shoulders and tightened his grasp as she stiffened. 'No, it's too late now. If you didn't want to talk to me you should have run straight away. But then you never could make snap decisions, could you, Gerda? But you *are* cold, trembling....' He began to rub his hand slowly up and down her arm, his warmth hard against the silk of her sleeve. 'Why didn't you put a wrap on?'

'I—I came out to get cool,' she said wildly. 'Jordan, I want to talk to you. I——'

'Talk away. I'm here.'

'Yes, but——' She gripped at the back of the seat till her knuckles gleamed white. His closeness was destroying all coherent thought and the instinct to flee conflicted wildly with the urge to stay. 'Not here. Not if...'

'Not if what?' He was turning her to face him, enfolding his arms more closely and making her own arms imprisoned against his chest so that she could only clasp her hands and look up at him with despair in her eyes.

The dark and silver sky reflected in the window beyond Jordan's shoulder supplied her answer. She made small despairing movements with her hands. 'We can be seen. Stuart will see, and——'

'I don't think that matters. It might be a very good idea.' Jordan's eyes compelled her to hold his gaze. 'A spark of jealousy, awareness of desire ... it's worth anything to make my brother desire a return to normal life. So why not? You're still my ally, Gerda, surely?'

Inexorably he drew her closer, the tilt of his head making plain his intention. His mouth curved but did not hurry to claim her own, and for an agonised moment it came to her that he was fully aware of his dangerous power, that he knew her body had become a fluid, aching desire for him.

Self-knowledge gave the impetus to summon the last vestige of pride and she turned her head. 'No,' she whispered, 'I'm not your ally—not a weapon in your hands to hurt Stuart. I won't. Let me go!'

He laughed softly at the slender hands thrusting impotently against his chest. 'But I don't want to let you go. I like your melodramatic little analogy. A weapon. Slender, almost as cold as steel, but not quite strong enough.'

The hands locked behind her waist felt like steel, pitiless in their strength as they pinned her against his hard body. She fought vainly, trying to evade his mouth. 'No!' she choked. 'Don't you remember what you said? Outside Toby's? That night——'

'What did I say?'

'That you'd have to be screaming for a woman be- fore—before——' Her voice cracked and she arched back against his arms, too distraught now to realise that resistance only inflamed him.

'That was then—this is now,' he said in dangerously silky tones. 'You always had a certain appeal to the senses, Gerda. A challenge difficult for any man to re- sist.'

'I never tried to challenge you.'

'No? Look at me, Gerda. Unless you're afraid to.'

The softly spoken taunt stilled her, and weakness came on a great wave.

He said, 'I remember two certain occasions when you came into my arms willingly enough. I even got the impression you found me attractive. Have I changed so much?'

Still she tried to resist, tried to stem the force of longing he had unleashed, before the weapons of de- spair and disillusion became too frail. 'You'll never change,' she whispered brokenly. 'You only use people to achieve *your* aims. You're hard, and—and ruthless, and——'

'Am I?' His dark gaze did not flicker a fraction, nor did his tone change. 'Because I admit wanting to make love to you?'

'Love! Love doesn't come into it—not with you,' she choked. 'You don't know what it means. If—if you wanted to make love to a woman why did you send Diane away?'

His mouth thinned. 'Because I didn't happen to feel like making love to Diane,' he said insolently.

She recoiled in sick loathing, hardly able to believe

111

that even he could be capable of such callousness. A violent trembling seized her limbs and she stared up at him with pain-filled eyes.

'You're despicable! I hate you! *How I hate you!*'

His arms slackened, fell away, and for a dreadful moment she thought he would strike her. Then he gave a twisted smile that somehow inflicted greater pain than any blow. 'So I'm despicable. You don't change, Gerda.'

For long moments he stared down into her frozen face, then he said slowly: 'I wonder which one of us is the true defamer. Come with me. There's something you should see.'

A chill fear spread through her, holding her immobile, and he gave an impatient exclamation. 'You needn't stand there like a ravaged innocent. You know too well how to bestow the kiss of death on any man's desire.'

Wordlessly she moved forward, hardly able to see where she stepped for the hot tears scalding her eyes. His steps crunched dully, and she flinched when he brushed against her shoulder as he held open the garden door that led into his study.

It was dim within and the shadows seemed to hold hidden menace. She stood on the threshold, afraid of what might be to come and aware in her feverish brain that the menace lay in Jordan himself. He moved heavily, a dark outline reaching for a switch near the desk, and then the glow touched his head to silvery steel. He picked up the decanter and splashed whisky into a tumbler. There was a savageness in his movements and in the way he turned and thrust the drink at her.

'No, thank you. I——'

'Suit yourself.' He raised the tumbler to his own lips.

She said, 'What is it? If it's anything to do with your impossible idea I don't want to listen. I'm through. I'm not going to be drawn into your schemes. I'm not going to see Stuart any more. I'm not going to try to talk him into doing anything against his will. He's suffered enough already.' Her voice rose wildly. 'I won't! You can't make me, do you hear?'

He gave no indication of having heard. He was rummaging in a black briefcase on the desk top, hauling out papers and files, till he found what he sought and drew it out.

It was a large, stiff manilla folder of the envelope type. He opened it and spilled out the contents. There were photographs, colour, thin yellow sheets of notes, blank sheets of glossy papers of varying sizes, and what looked like an artist's layout for some cover or something.

Jordan straightened. His profile was controlled, almost expressionless.

'Do you remember these?'

Her lips felt stiff, unable to frame an evasive response while her heart thudded so fiercely she could hear its anguish.

'Take a look.' He indicated the pile on the desk with a careless wave of his hand.

'Where did you get them?'

'They landed on my desk on Friday—from our agency.'

His voice sounded a long way away. He picked up one of the photographs and held it up, his eyes narrowed critically, picked up another with his left hand, appraised them in turn, then laid them on the folder.

Gerda closed her eyes and groped for the support of a chair back. Through his eyes those strange and beautiful photographs damned her and flooded her with shame. How had he found them? How could she ever expect him to understand that there was a story behind those sea-mist studies, or how deep was the anguish behind the decision forced on her four long years ago? What dreadful retribution was he planning to enact now?

He glanced at her, seemingly unmoved by her tragic despair, and said carelessly: 'Aphrodite—then and now. I must admit your charm, even though it was slightly immature.' He reached for his half finished drink. 'Tell me, does it take a great deal of courage for a girl to do this kind of thing? To let the camera's eye reveal and capture her for the world to see? Despite the artistic swirls of spume—one can almost hear the cries of the sea-birds and those breakers crashing and the mist, this naked little sea-sprite is you. I must salute the cameraman, whoever he is, he's undoubtedly an artist,' he added dryly.

'He swore no one would recognise me,' she said brokenly. 'They were for a special assignment—he said he didn't want a professional model—none of them were right—he——'

'Only *your* youth and innocence? You flatter yourself.'

'I hated myself. He begged me, offered me a fantastic fee. I was rude to him, then—then something happened. I—I had to get the money. I——' Suddenly her voice failed her and she fought for control. Jordan's dark satanic features swam in a haze and she dashed her hand fiercely across her eyes. 'Why have you got them? Why?'

'They're among a series sent for approval for our next calendar'—the way he spoke brought fresh waves of hot colour to her face—'there's been the usual argument over feminine appeal versus Highland scenery.

Somebody remembered the old Internationale effort—
it became quite famous on the Continent, though they
didn't distribute it in this country.'

'And you ... you mean ...?' she stretched out a
trembling hand, 'Wentford want to ...?'

'That's the general idea—subject to my okay, of
course.'

Horror overwhelmed her. She thought of her
mother, of her quiet dignified stepfather whom she'd
met only twice since her mother's second marriage, and
of the bitterness of the sacrifice that had brought it
about.

She whispered unbelievingly: 'You wouldn't?'

'What makes you think I wouldn't?'

Her head bowed and she let her hands fall to her
sides. Why should she expect mercy from Jordan
Black?

'I'm ruthless. I'm despicable,' he said coldly. 'It's a
business matter. A commodity you sold four years ago.
Why shouldn't I make use of it?'

The implication was crystal clear. This was Jordan
Black's second card.

CHAPTER VI

THE clash with Jordan had drained Gerda's strength until she was trembling on the verge of illness. She found herself outside the door of her room without conscious memory of getting there, and in the depths of her subconscious was the need of a restorative, a drink, the only thing her distraught brain could suggest to still the shuddering of despair. But not for anything could she return downstairs in search of the anodyne alcohol was reputed to provide. All she wanted was to be alone. . . .

She thrust at the half-open door, and fell back before the small determined figure of Rachel Lammond.

'Sooner than I expected. Good. I thought you might be hitting the pillow with Jordan.' Rachel went back to the dent he had obviously made in Gerda's bed and sat down on the crumpled coverlet. She looked defiantly at Gerda's white face and said calmly: 'I want to talk to you.'

'Not now—please.' For a moment she could not even retaliate against the crude implication in the younger girl's greeting. 'I—I've got an appalling headache.'

As she said it she realised it was true; her head was throbbing unbearably and she felt cold and sick. She went to the fitted basin in the corner and splashed water over her face, dabbing it dry and uncaring of smudged make-up.

'You do look pretty dished.' Rachel considered her with dispassionate eyes. 'You're not going to pass out or anything, are you?'

'No,' Gerda said dully. She sat down at the dressing table and reached for her tissues. Applying cleanser with apathetic movements, she avoided Rachel's gaze through the mirror. 'What do you want?'

'To know exactly what game you're playing.'

Game! Gerda sighed. A scene with Rachel would be the final humiliation. She said wearily: 'Please say whatever you want to say and then leave me. I feel dreadful.'

'How do you think I feel?' Rachel flashed. 'What did you come back for?'

'Because I was invited.'

'That's not true. You came because Jordan wants to break it up between Stuart and me, and he thinks you can do the breaking. Well, you can't, and if you're wise you won't try. You didn't want Stuart three years ago, so you don't want him now.' Rachel's cheeks had taken on a feverish colour and she stood up. 'Go away and leave us alone.'

'Listen,' Gerda swung round on the stool and faced the tempestuous girl, 'try to believe me, I only want Stuart to be happy. I want to do what's best for his future.'

'I can do that. I love him.'

'I know you do. So do I, though I doubt if you'll understand how.'

'I understand all right,' Rachel said bitterly. 'You're the same as all the others. You only want what you consider best for Stuart, not what he wants. You're all too blind to see what I see.'

There was a curious ring of truth in Rachel's words, a germ of something not yet glimpsed yet holding conviction. More gently, she said: 'There isn't any question or mystery about what is best for Stuart. The one essential thing is that Stuart takes the chance of being able to walk again.'

'Yes, but he won't take it while Jordan, and you, and everybody else tries to bulldoze him into taking it. There is a risk. Stuart might die.'

'Stuart won't die. He's young and strong and he has courage.'

'That's what they all say.' Rachel sank down on the bed and shook her head impatiently. 'Can't you realise that he's frightened? He needs understanding and something strong enough to overcome that fear.'

'I should have thought that the desire to walk again would be strong enough to overcome fear.' Gerda turned back to the mirror and put her hand to her eyes. 'Do you really think you can succeed where everyone else has failed?'

'Yes, if people will leave me alone to succeed in my own way.'

Gerda sighed. 'Doesn't the decision ultimately rest with Stuart himself? I don't think any of us can force him. His own mother is against the idea, and if she influences him . . .'

'And that's another thing,' Rachel cried. 'If you hadn't come back on the scene and interfered it might have been different.'

'Oh, for goodness' sake! How can a couple of weekends make all that difference?'

'Mrs Black's away on holiday, on a cruise. I persuaded Stuart not to go with her, so that we could have a whole month on our own,' Rachel flared. 'If you hadn't landed back and unsettled him we might have been married by now.'

'Married!' Gerda gestured despairingly. 'Did you think Jordan would ever let you get away with that? He——'

'I know exactly what Jordan thinks, and I shall win.

118

I've got it all worked out. Stuart and I will——'

'Yes, but suppose you do. Then what? How are you going to look after Stuart? Where will you live?' Rising irritation with what she thought was sheer adolescent immaturity sharpened Gerda's voice. 'Have you the slightest idea of what it means to cope with a crippled person? You're crazy even to think of it.'

'I'm not.' The cool assurance of the younger girl made Gerda look sharply over her shoulder. 'I suppose you'll go and blab it all to Jordan if I tell you, but it'll work out, never you fear.'

For a moment Gerda stared at her, then she said bitterly, 'Jordan's the last person I'd blab to, but don't tell me if you don't want to.'

'I do, because I want you to understand.' Rachel came to sit in a cane chair near the dressing table. She looked imploringly at the older girl. 'I want Stuart to marry me in secret. We're of age. No one can stop us. I think Leon would help over the purely practical matters like getting Stuart to Eastbourne for the actual ceremony, but if he won't I'll find somebody who will. Then we simply come back here and tell no one.'

'Yes, but it isn't as easy as that.'

'I'm not finished yet. And I'm quite aware of everything it means. It would be a proper marriage. Being crippled didn't make Stuart impotent, you know,' Rachel said frankly, 'so there wouldn't be any chance for Jordan to try and have the marriage annulled. He couldn't do a thing, except throw us out, and I don't think he'd do that. If he did ... Well, I'd think of something. I have an allowance—my father's too stinking rich for his own good—but I'd work day and night for Stuart if I had to. That doesn't worry me.'

An unwilling admiration was growing in Gerda. Whatever faults Rachel might have she had courage, and she meant every word she said. Gerda said gently, 'And then?'

'Then Stuart will have the operation.'

'He might not. Have you faced that possibility?'

'No. Don't you see? If I marry him, and perhaps get pregnant, he'll have a tremendous incentive. It's the only way. If I marry him as he is now, it'll convince him that his being crippled doesn't make any difference to the way I feel about him. He'll want to walk again, because I'll have given him the faith he needs.'

Gerda's eyes began to smart. There was something wonderful and very moving in Rachel's own steadfast faith and love. She said unsteadily, 'You love him very much.'

'Of course I love him. I've loved him for three years, and I've never wanted to look at another man. I've had to fight Jordan, fight my parents, deceive them, hurt them, because of loving Stuart. And there's something else,' Rachel looked down and her eyes were hidden, 'Stuart and I share something that will bind us together until we die. We can't escape it and I don't want to. That's why we have to marry and share the rest of our lives, whatever happens.'

The room misted. Gerda looked unseeingly into the mirror and for a moment the veils of the years parted. This was not the moment to tell of the secret she herself shared with Stuart. The telling would accomplish nothing, therefore it was better that it should remain untold.

Abruptly Rachel got to her feet and the turbulent nature Gerda knew was defying her again. 'So go away and don't come back. Stuart doesn't love you now. I know he once did, but it's dead now. As dead as a doornail. And you don't love him either.'

Gerda sighed. There was little she could say, little

she wanted to say. Jordan's plan had been doomed from the start. She had known it in her heart and had failed to argue. But how could she . . .?.

'If you don't leave him alone,' Rachel went on, 'I shall tell him.'

'Tell him what?' For a moment Gerda was lost in the bewilderment of her own thoughts. 'What can you tell Jordan?'

'I said I'll tell Stuart what I saw tonight. You and Jordan out on the terrace.' Rachel's mouth curved with scorn. 'No wonder he gave poor Diane the brush-off!'

She saw the shock on Gerda's parted mouth and shrugged. 'Oh, I couldn't care less which of you Jordan amuses himself with. Go ahead and cut Diane out if you can, but leave us alone.' She stood silent for a moment, then moved towards the door. 'You needn't worry. It'll work out all right.'

For both their sakes, Gerda hoped, but did not speak the thought aloud. Of her own she was beyond thinking. That would come later. Now she was only conscious of a strange relief that in some way responsibility had been taken from her shoulders. Now that she had glimpsed the real Rachel she felt humbled. She had made the same error of judgement as Jordan—or perhaps she had allowed herself to be unduly influenced by his judgement. Rachel was not the wild immature adolescent they had believed her to be. Perhaps once, but not now. She was deep, and remarkably clearsighted, and despite her youth she was more mature than Gerda herself felt at present.

She looked at the small intense girl in the flamboyant tunic suit and tiers of fat glossy amber beads, and suddenly she felt immeasurably old and inept, without wisdom.

Rachel was hesitating, twisting at the long loop of

beads, as though uncertain how to bring the meeting to an end. 'Well ...' she laid her hand on the door panel and trailed it down, 'I'd better be going.'

'Wait. Rachel, will you do something for me?'

'Depends what it is.'

Gerda looked down. 'I'd like to leave early in the morning, to go back by train, only ...' she raised her head and met Rachel's stare quite steadily, 'I've no idea of the train times, or how I get to the station from here.'

'That's easy.' Rachel relaxed. 'I'll take you myself.'

It was easier than Gerda had dared to dream. Rachel seemed to divine the undercurrents of despair in Gerda and sense that they were linked with Jordan Black. She landed up with a tray of tea and toast and a somewhat overdone egg a few minutes before seven the following morning and bade Gerda to get a move on. Gerda obeyed; she had no wish to be confronted by Jordan before she escaped, and less than twenty minutes later Rachel was driving her to the station, where she waited to see Gerda on to the train.

When it drew in Gerda held out her hand, then impulsively kissed Rachel on her cheek. 'It will work out—very soon, I hope. I'm glad now you told me—and thanks.'

'Don't mench,' said Rachel with a return to her offhand way. 'I'll tell Jordan you've gone.'

Gerda nodded numbly and got into a compartment. The sense of relief was still there, in that the issue of Stuart and his future had been taken out of her hands before she could contemplate grasping it, but it was dwarfed by the sense of inadequacy Rachel had evoked and the shadow of Jordan. Nothing was resolved, yet everything was resolved, because she had lost the desire to swim against the tide of despair.

The train gathered speed and the pale eastern sun poured through the window, bathing her wan face with a brilliance that failed to warm her. Now she was alone and enclosed with that despair, and the rhythm of the wheels hammered out the questions she could not answer. The contract ... Jordan's reaction to her alliance with Rachel ... the end of the final heart-breaking punishment he had inflicted on her last night. ... Round and round in circles, stripping off the outer layers of pain, centring remorselessly on the man at the core of it all, exposing the bitter quintessence of torment....

All through the sleepless hours of the night she had relived that scene in Jordan Black's room over and over again, trying to convince herself it was a dreadful nightmare. He couldn't be so cruel as to use those sea mist studies she had almost succeeded in forgetting during the four long lost years since they were taken. Surely he couldn't be so insensitive as to use them in their worst possible context, emblazoning them to the world and tarnishing the sacrifice they represented merely to satisfy his warped desire for revenge.

At last the contract, Howard, Stuart, and Rachel, the photographs all paled against this fresh agony. What did they matter? What did anything matter beside the damning cruelty of Jordan's final words last night?

A business matter. A commodity. Something to be used.

A man without mercy. *And yet she had to love him!*

*   *   *

The next two days seemed endless. She was constantly tensed for an angry communication from Jordan Black, but nothing came. Merrick eyed her dispassionately when she arrived at the office and remarked succinctly: 'You must feel the way I look,' then, giving her a second, sharper glance, added, 'Forget it. I ought to remember that girls don't have hangovers—only headaches.'

She could summon only a ghost of a smile in response to his bluff effort at humour, and he scratched his head. 'Why don't you take the day off? You know there isn't a lot for you to do when Howard isn't here.'

She refused, knowing that day-to-day living had to go on and that in her present state of mind leisure was the last thing she wanted. Leisure meant a mind unoccupied.... 'I think I'll turn out the big filing cabinet in Howard's office,' she said, getting up. 'I'm sure there's a lot of old stuff that could be burnt.'

The self-appointed task filled most of the morning, even though she did not linger over it—the shadowy presence of Howard was too potent and the empty office too poignant a reminder of strength missing where it had too long been taken for granted. Merrick wandered in once to see how she was getting on, and perhaps that nebulous sense of missing strength infected him too, for he said suddenly: 'Leave that—I've a notion to write to Black.'

Suddenly wishing she hadn't refused his suggestion that she take the day off, she followed him into his small office.

'I'm fed-up with all this shilly-shallying—we never played this game of nerves in the old days,' he observed sourly. 'Who the hell does Black think he is? God Almighty or something?'

He dictated the letter and she typed it. Merrick's style was brusque and to the point, and she wondered what Jordan would say when the letter reached him. It was a futile effort, of that she was certain, and for a moment she experienced a wild impulse to doctor the letter...

Dear Sir,
   Perhaps it will influence your decision if we inform you of the dismissal of Mrs Manston, owing to her gross negligence over the negotiations we entrusted her with regarding...

No, 'mishandling' would be a better substitute for 'negligence'....

Merrick coughed, and she fought down the almost hysterical impulse. She checked the letter and Merrick signed it without reading it over. 'We'll see what that brings—if anything.'

It looked as though his half-hearted surmise would prove justified as the week dragged on without bringing any acknowledgement from Wentfords. Nor was there any word from Stuart. The phone calls had ceased, and she could only wonder and wait, until lengthening silence would start the hope that it was all over and she could begin trying to forget. But scornful instinct denied the hope....

The one gleam of lightness in the week came on the Thursday evening. At last Howard was nearing the end of his stay in hospital. He raised his hand with a cheerful wave of greeting when she entered the small side ward and grinned happily.

'Next week. Probably Monday,' he informed her when she was settled in the hard green chair by the bedside. 'They're making the arrangements tomorrow to transfer me to the convalescent home.'

'I'm so glad,' she said tremulously.

'So much for their predictions of it being weeks before I got on my feet again,' he said with the first return of his former vigour. 'Mind, I had the devil of an argument with them.' He began to recount the argument word by word, until Gerda waved an admonishing hand.

'You're getting too excited. Don't spoil it.'

'And don't you start on me as well!' He sank back against his pillows and gave a deep sigh, watching her with a tired, intent regard that held a strong light of affection. She sensed that he was lapsing into that air of abstraction which overtakes the sick person once the mending process begins, as though the mind has to pause frequently to recharge, and she stayed silent until he blinked and gave a small wry smile.

'Was I staring, my dear? I'm sorry.'

'No, not at all. You just looked delightfully lazy.'

'Did I? I was thinking how like your mother you are.' He paused. 'Does it irritate a daughter to be told she resembles her mother? I seem to recollect saying it before. Naturally I mean when she was the age you are now. She was very beautiful, you know.'

'She still is,' Gerda said quietly.

'Is she happy?'

'I think so,' Gerda said more cautiously.

'I could never imagine her settling down abroad and marrying a scholarly man—a philosopher and historian of all men. She was always such a party girl, loved being with bright people. Perhaps her illness changed her.'

'I think it did.'

'That was one of the biggest regrets of my life,' he said slowly, 'that I was in Australia when she needed the help I could have gladly given. I've never quite forgiven you for not telling me, you know.'

'How could I?' Gerda traced the pattern in the white

embossed coverlet. 'You were so far away. I couldn't ask you.'

'I would have come back.'

'From Australia? Don't you think you did enough for my father? I know you would have helped. Many a time I wished with all my heart that you were near.'

'And yet you didn't call on me.'

She looked down, and they were silent for a while, each far away in their own thoughts. Then he stirred and looked at her shadowed face.

'I wanted to marry her. More than any other woman I've known. First when she was hardly out of her teens, but your father won. Later, when she was widowed, I wanted to take care of you both, but she just couldn't feel that way about me.'

He lapsed back into silence and she watched him, the lights of reflection in her eyes. Howard Durrel might have been her father, but fate had decreed otherwise. He had never married, and now it was extremely unlikely that he ever would. She could not help reflecting on the quirk of fate that made a man love a woman to the exclusion of all others, even though she would never be his. The same quirk that decreed that she should lose her own heart to a man who scorned her very existence, to the extent that he would go out of his way to hurt her....

She came out of her reverie to Howard's musing voice and his mention of Blaise's name.

'... worries me at times. You need someone to care for you. You're not hard enough to be a career woman. Isn't there anyone to take Blaise's place?'

'No, no one at all. I—I've no desire to marry again.'

'You sound as though you were disillusioned with marriage. You were happy with Blaise, weren't you?'

'Perfectly.' She avoided his eyes and he said quickly:

'I'm sorry, I'm intruding. I forget I have no right to interfere or advise on your personal life, but please, my dear, I'd like to think that you would come to me if ever you were troubled.'

'But of course I would. Didn't I come to you, and you made a place in Charingfolds for me? When I'd almost forgotten my training and my shorthand was so rusty my pencil squeaked in sympathy?' She swallowed hard. 'You're the one we are worried about, so just concentrate on yourself for once and let's see you home again,' she whispered.

'I shall be back by the end of the month, and that's a promise.'

'Just make sure you keep it.'

With a sense of relief she heard the discreet sound of a bell and knew it signified the end of the visiting hour. Howard's kindliness acted like a catalyst on her bruised emotions and brought her dangerously near to loss of control—the last thing she wanted in the circumstances.

'Oh——' He remembered something as she was on the point of departing. 'There are a few things I'll need before Monday.' He leaned over to hunt in the bedside locker. 'I made a note of them ... if you would ask Mrs Sanders, in case she doesn't have time to visit me before then.'

Gerda tucked the list in her bag and after promising to see to it and to visit him again on the Sunday before he was transferred to the convalescent home in the country she decided to make a detour on her way home and pass on his instructions to his housekeeper.

Mrs Sanders tended to be garrulous. She pressed Gerda to stay for a cup of coffee, and by the time Gerda got back to the flat the day was almost over. She made mechanical preparations for the morning, set out her breakfast things under a traycloth, laid out fresh undies, went through the nightly attention to hair and skin, and tried to keep Jordan's face out of her memory....

*   *   *

For the first time in six months she slept in the following morning and was over an hour late for work. She rushed, worried because she was by nature a conscientious person and because at her job she had never allowed herself to take advantage of her privileged relationship with her boss. There was a strong breeze, almost a gale, that morning and a remarkable dearth of Northridge buses to further impede her progress.

In her hurry to tidy the windblown traces from her hair when she reached Charingfolds she did not at first notice an unusually quiet air about the main building. For once the muted racket of typewriters from the general office had lulled and the clatter of the canteen trolley, which had usually begun its round for the morning break by now, was missing. As Gerda hurried along from the cloakroom she could see through the glass partition of the accounts office. The girls were clustered in a group in one corner, talking among themselves, but Mr Jamieson and the new young sales manager were also in there, looking vaguely worried. There must be a flap on in Accounts, Gerda decided, opening the door of Howard's office and glancing in before she went next door to report to Merrick.

There was a buzz of voices within and before Gerda could tap and enter the supervisor of the general office emerged, a quiet middle-aged woman called Elizabeth Smythe with whom Gerda was on friendly terms.

She also wore the same vaguely worried expression the men in Accounts had worn and she gave a negative gesture with one hand.

'I shouldn't go in for a moment.'

'Why not?' Gerda stared. 'What's happened?'

'I'm not sure—yet. But something's up,' Elizabeth returned. 'Nobody ever tells me anything round here, but all I know is that I've to keep out all interruptions.'

Gerda frowned. 'Who's in there?'

'Mr Taylor and Mr Merrick and one of the other directors. We might as well go and have our tea while we wait.'

'I've just arrived—broken my good record.' Gerda bit her lip and tried to think what could be happening. She had a sudden dark tremor of doubt. 'It isn't anything to do with Mr Durrel . . .?'

'Not as far as I know.'

Gerda relaxed. 'I'd better see to the post.'

'You can't. It's in there,' Elizabeth gestured at the closed door, 'I had the same idea.'

It was strange how a sensation of disaster could paralyse an entire department, she reflected uneasily as she accompanied Elizabeth along to her small room adjoining the main office. They drank their coffee, tacitly refraining from surmises which could be totally inaccurate, but each of them inwardly worried.

At last they heard firm footsteps down the corridor and from the window saw Mr Taylor and his companion getting into their cars. Gerda turned from the window. 'I can't stand this any longer. I'm going to find out what *is* going on.'

'Don't forget to come back and tell me,' Elizabeth said in resigned tones, returning to her desk. As she reached it her desk phone buzzed and she pounced on it. Gerda hesitated, saw the older woman nod towards her, and slipped from the room.

She found Merrick sunk in gloom and staring mournfully into an empty whisky tumbler. He looked up and for a moment his eyes retained their blankness. She faltered, 'What's happened?'

'Taylor senior's pulling out.'

'Old Mr Taylor? Not out of Charingfolds!' Gerda came to a standstill.

'Yes. After all these years. We just heard this morning.'

'But he can't! He holds a third of——'

'He can,' said Merrick flatly, 'and he is.'

She moved forward and dismay slowed her steps. 'I can't believe it. What are you going to do?'

'I'm calling an emergency meeting of the board. It'll have to be Monday—damn the weekend!—we can't do it before then. I want you to contact them immediately. If you can't locate them in person by phone find out where you can. Send telegrams if necessary, but they've got to be here Monday. Then you can take a look at *this*.'

He flipped through the untidy sprawl of papers on the desk and pulled out a single sheet. He tossed it across towards her, and the distinctive grey and green embossing of Wentfords' letter-heading leapt to her gaze. The paper felt stiff and cold between her suddenly nerveless fingers, and the premonition of fresh disaster was upon her long before her eye could transmit the curt, impersonal sentences to her brain.

Thank you for your letter of the fifteenth inst. In view of the results of certain investigations I have made and pending the outcome of other negotiations at present in hand, I regret I must postpone my decision on the renewal of the supply contract between Charingfolds and our new subsidiary, the firm formerly known as Van-Lorn Electronics Ltd. I regret any inconvenience this delay may have caused and wish to assure you that it in no way reflects the slightest dissatisfaction on your previous transactions with Van-Lorn. Please convey my sincerest wishes to Mr Durrel for his speedy and complete recovery. Yours ...

The signature was firm and clear. Jordan Black *would* use ink as black as his name, she thought bitterly, scanning the letter with smarting, angry eyes. His 'sincerest' wishes were an insult. It was brutal. It ...

'The last straw, isn't it?' said Merrick.

Gerda shook her head, not trusting herself to speak. He got up and took the letter from her, his mouth compressing. He walked across to the window and stared at the cars nosed against the cool green lawn verges. He said slowly, 'I wonder if there's any chance of getting Howard along on Monday before they whip him down to Hampshire. He'd want to be here, and he ought to be here. When he hears about Taylor, and see this....'

The letter rustled softly as it fell on the desk top and Merrick swung round. 'You saw him last night, didn't you? What do you think?'

She *was* thinking, wildly and fearfully, and she took small frantic steps forward. 'No! He—he—— I don't think we should. I don't think we should tell him.'

'But damn it, he's got to know! We can't keep all this from him. He'd be furious if we did. You don't know what you're saying, girl.'

'Yes, but it'll be a shock. The one thing's bad enough, but two setbacks like these. Don't you understand?' she pleaded. 'This could undo all the good of his treatment. The doctors said he hadn't to be worried. He's going to be worried to death over all this.'

'I know he is, but what else can we do?' Merrick ran his hand over his thinning hair. 'What do you suggest?'

The note of sarcasm hardly stung at all; there was too much hurt already. She said helplessly, 'I don't know. I wish I did. Couldn't we wait till the meeting's over? See what happens, and then tell him about that, and——'

'And what about the other?' Merrick jingled coins in his pocket and stared at her. 'No, it's no use, Gerda. I know you're fond of him and all that sort of thing, but this is the wrong time for sentiment. It's business and he has to know.'

She was silent, knowing in her heart that there was no other answer, yet some instinct crying inside her and warning . . .

Merrick said, 'I'd better go along and see him to-night. Get it over with. Are you coming with me?'

'No, don't. I—I've had another idea. I——' She looked at the hateful white oblong on the desk and then up at Merrick's impatient expression. 'Give me a day. Till tomorrow.'

'What can you do, for God's sake? You can't do anything!'

'I can. I'm going to see Jordan Black. I can't do anything about the other thing, but I might . . .' She gave a long shuddering sigh. 'I'm going to ask Jordan Black to change his mind.'

Merrick snorted. 'Does that read like a man who'd change his mind?'

'No. But I've got to try. I've got to try,' she repeated.

CHAPTER VII

ONCE the decision was made ·pride and stubbornness would not allow cowardice to effect a reversal. A strange block in Gerda's subconscious mind shut out everything except the actual moments that were building up to those moments she could not foresee, nor could she consciously plan ahead to any practical formula. When she was finally ready to set off her bedroom was a shambles of decided-against dresses, blouses, shoes, and feminine clutter. Lipsticks without caps, pieces of jewellery, a wispy scarf, and an upset bottle of hand lotion littered the dressing table top, yet somehow she had emerged flawlessly groomed without any memory of doing so or the faintest idea of how she looked.

She could only think that she hadn't the faintest idea of where she was going or if she would find Jordan Black when she got there. She had vague recollections that he had a flat in town, somewhere.... The telephone directory yielded the address—Innescourt Mews —she'd better get a taxi—she'd never find Innescourt Mews—but she would not try telephoning. What would she say?

She still hadn't the remotest idea of how she would begin to explain herself when the taxi deposited her at the narrow cobbled entrance to one of the rare enchanting remnants of old London that still hid, as though they were afraid of discovery, among the new and the white and the soaring towers of glass that reached for the sky. The late sun shone on the polished cobbles and reflected small inky half-hoops of shadows among them as she looked at the jealously guarded conversions of eighteenth-century London. There were lattices and window-boxes and coach lamps over the old porches, and she wondered if she had been mistaken; this surround was totally out of character—Jordan Black's character. He belonged in a penthouse atop one of those soaring towers of concrete and glass, not in this Georgian gem facing her at the end of the cobbled lane. There was a very small discreet plate with his name and a bell, and her courage almost failed her. He wouldn't be here. It was Friday; he would have gone down to Green Rigg for the weekend.

She walked slowly round the angle of the house, and in the hidden recess she saw the end of the car protruding, dark green, and the star shape on the hub-cap. She stood there, caught in the turmoil of indecision, and above her head Jordan Black's voice said:

'The door's on the latch.'

She started, and from the open window he looked down on her upturned face. His dark brows were raised, and the wind was catching the thick ruffle of steely hair. He said, 'I presume you were wandering down here in search of me?'

Without speaking she turned back. The door gave to her touch, as he had said, and opened into a low arched hall, shadowy turquoise and amber parquet, with a closed door facing her and a narrow stairway to her right. She hesitated, let the door swing softly behind her as though cutting off her escape, and slowly ascended the stairs.

There were old Japanese prints at shoulder height, but she did not see them, and the stairway rose straight from its halfway bend into a long spacious living room. He had not moved from the window.

He said, 'Well, come in. Unless you're getting to sit

on the stairs and make small talk.'

She moved as far as a dark green leather Jeroboam chair and stopped. 'I—I shut the door downstairs.'

'How momentous!' At last he moved. 'What would you like to drink?'

'Nothing, thank you.'

'Do sit down. Cigarette?'

'No, thank you—were you going out?'

'No—I do stay at home occasionally.' He dropped into a chair and crossed elegantly grey-clad legs, apparently not a whit put out by her unexpected arrival. He regarded her tensely upright figure perched uneasily on the very edge of the deep chair, and smiled slightly. 'Well, this is an unexpected pleasure.'

He waited, not making it easy for her, and she gazed round the tastefully furnished lounge as though it might provide her with the inspiration to begin the plea that refused to become the right words. He watched her, pressing his thumb idly against his bottom lip, then followed her glance to the high domed niches with their softly concealed lighting at either side of the green marble fireplace. He stood up. 'But of course ... women always like a conducted tour of houses they haven't been in before. Come, I'll show you round.'

'We'll go downstairs first. Actually, I didn't do this conversion, if I had I would have sacrificed the small garden space at the back.... The garage robs space under here, and I dislike the vogue for kitchenette-diners. So I use this downstairs living room as a dining room. One of these days I'll get round to ripping this pine panelling out of the kitchen—it's quite spacious and attractive—old American style—but to me it strikes a false note against the period of the place.'

He lounged against the big fridge while she looked

at the pine units and stainless steel that added up to a picture out of an ideal-kitchen catalogue. Then he led the way through the small dining room and upstairs, to glib commentaries on blending the best of old with the functionalism of new, until he stopped abruptly, blocking out a glimpse of a topaz and sepia fitted bathroom, and faced her. 'You know perfectly well you haven't heard a word I said. Why did you come?'

She took a deep breath. 'I came to ask you to reconsider your decision.'

'Which one?'

'You know which one.' Her voice was tightly controlled. 'We got your letter today.'

'Oh, so this is a business call,' he said dryly.

'No, it isn't. Your letter was the most heartless——' She bit back the words which would betray emotion and tried to stay calm. 'I came to ask you for logical, valid reasons against renewing the contract, and exactly what you mean by these investigations and negotiations which are pending.'

'I think you know them already.'

'If I knew I wouldn't be asking.'

'Very well.' He led the way back into the lounge and went to the drinks tray. 'I'm considering a bid for Charingfolds.'

'What? You?'

'Why not? They would make a useful ancillary.'

'But Charingfolds isn't for sale. Howard wouldn't dream of letting it go, and he has the controlling interest. It's not possible that——'

'I think it is.' He came towards her with the two glasses. 'I know about Taylor. I know quite a few things which point to the possibility. For one thing, I don't think Durrel will try to hold on. I doubt very much if he'll want to when he gets over this bout.'

'Yes, he will. How long have you had this in mind?' she demanded sharply.

'Quite a while.' He sat down on the studio couch and looked at her with impervious calm. 'For several weeks.'

'All that time? And you never told me?'

'The time wasn't ripe.'

'I—I can't believe it.' She felt shaken and cold, unable to comprehend what this would mean. Suddenly the wild thoughts broke free and presented the only conclusion that made emotional sense. She looked at him with frightened eyes. 'Are you doing this because of—because of Stuart and Rachel and because I——'

'I'm a businessman and I'm considering only the business angle,' he said curtly. 'Charingfolds are shaky. They could go down. At their present rate they will. I could put them on their feet again and make them a profitable subsidiary of Wentford.'

'Just like that,' she said dully. 'Just business and profit. Not people and endeavour and consideration for their feelings.'

He shrugged, and the weight of failure dragged at her shoulders. For long moments she was silent, then she sighed and stood up. She had been foolish even to imagine that she might accomplish anything by this impulsive visit; crazy even to believe that she might influence Jordan Black to show the slightest trace of softening. He was hard and insensitive all the way through, and she was the last person who would ever cause him to change.

With his cold courtesy he held her light linen jacket, and, about to turn to slip her arms into it, she hesitated and met his dark, unreadable glance. Her hands dropped. 'Jordan, please tell me. Be honest. Has all this had anything to do with me? Because I'm connected with Charingfolds, and there's been a long personal friendship between Howard and my family? I know how you feel about me, and Stuart, and—and everything,' she rushed on, 'but I've got to know. Would you allow your personal feelings to influence your business decisions?'

His hands slowly lowered the jacket. 'Supposing my answer was yes. What would you say?'

'I—I've tried to convince myself I'm mistaken, but I can't.' She shook her head despairingly. 'I don't know what to say, except—except that it's going to break Howard Durrel's heart, and hurt a lot of people's lives, all because I——' Her mouth trembled and she gave up the attempt to face his level stare. Slowly she took the jacket out of his hands and turned blindly away before he saw the tears brimming. She said unsteadily, 'I—I must go now. I——'

'Gerda.' The changed note in his voice checked her, but she did not turn. His steps vibrated softly and stopped. 'I don't understand you, Gerda. This intense loyalty to Durrel and the firm. It—it's almost abnormal in—in *you*.'

'In a woman, you mean.'

'In a woman I've found to be without any personal loyalty,' he flashed. 'Even now ... Oh, forget it,' he gestured impatiently, 'and for God's sake don't stand there looking at me like that! Like a martyr. As if I were to blame.'

'Aren't you?' she said bitterly.

'That, from you! How typical of a woman.' His mouth reformed its grim lines. 'Only a woman will take a stand on a lie and fight to the bitter end.'

'Fight! How can I fight?' she flashed. 'When you hold all the weapons. How can I fight on a lie when you refuse to listen to the truth? Right from the start you've believed the worst of me. You blamed me for your brother's accident. You tried to blackmail me into breaking up his affair with the girl who really loves him—but you hate her as well! You accuse me of disloyalty. You judged and condemned me without knowing the facts, and you insult me. Oh yes!' she cried as his eyes sparked angry denial. 'I haven't forgotten how you ferreted and vetted me three years ago—to see if I was good enough for your precious brother. He told me so himself. We—we——' her voice trembled, 'we thought it was funny then, but I'll never forget you. Never. All right! Hate me and punish me if you must, but don't make another man suffer. A man who deserves only the best life should give him.'

'Does he matter so much to you?'

'Yes, he matters!' Trembling and spent from the force of her outburst, she strove to cling to the vestiges of control. 'Don't do this because of *me*. Because it's cruel and unfair, and—and I can't bear it any more. I——'

He took a jerky step towards her. 'You've done your own share of condemning, Gerda. You—oh, don't weep! Why do women always——'

She shook her head, groped blindly for her handbag, trying to avert her distraught face. She started to shoulder into her jacket and was too blinded by tears to see.

He divined her instinct for flight and barred her way. 'You can't go out like that. You'll——'

'It doesn't matter. Oh, I knew you wouldn't listen. I——'

'Gerda! Don't——'

'I—I don't care—let me pass—you don't——'

'No.' He stayed unmoving at the head of the stairs. 'Gerda, I can't——' The impatient exclamation died and he caught at her shoulders, gripping them hard, as though his touch could magically bring calm.

Her mouth worked tremulously as she tried to evade him, and her jacket slid to the floor. She bent to scoop it up and collided with him. Clumsily he helped her to don it, tried to draw out the collar that had turned in at one side, and suddenly put his arms round her.

'Try to calm down. You're overwrought.'

She gave a shuddering sigh, and he said: 'You'd better come and sit down.'

'No,' her head turned convulsively, 'I don't want—I didn't mean to——'

'Don't talk.' His hands were hard and brusque, pressing her head against his shoulder. 'It's all been said.'

Her shoulders trembled. 'It hasn't. It——'

'Be quiet.'

His voice was firm, but gentler, even though his hands still restrained while she tried desperately to quell the aching turmoil of distress and gradually she perceived the subtle change in him. After a few moments he said, 'I suppose Howard sent you.'

'No, he didn't. He doesn't——' She swallowed hard. 'I didn't want him to know.'

He stayed silent, and his hand strayed to her hair, making the inborn motions of comfort a man makes almost automatically when a woman weeps. The awkward gestures moved over her cheek and they made her want to surrender to a fresh surge of tears. She was conscious of a great weakness pervading her body, as though she had scourged her spirit and left an empty vessel. Now she wanted to draw closer to him, invoke further comfort, somehow to draw into herself the strength he had taken from her. A tremor passed through her with the realisation and she knew she had to resist her own dangerous senses.

She stirred, and he responded, letting his grasp slacken so that she drew away a little, and looked down at her.

'All right?'

She gave an almost imperceptible downward movement of her head, unable to look at him, and he said in a strangely gruff voice:

'Gerda, even if I were to do as you ask—settle that contract business, forget about my plans for Charing-folds—do you believe it would resolve everything?'

'Resolve . . .? Of—of course it would,' she whispered unsteadily.

'Are you sure?'

'Yes—— I—I don't know what you mean.'

He sighed. 'I think you do. Gerda, look at me.'

For several moments she could not trust herself to obey without betraying herself, and he gave a small exclamation of impatience. 'Why don't you face it? For how much longer are you going to fight the inevitable?'

'But it isn't. You don't have to take over Charing——'

'I'm not talking about that!' He laid firm fingers along the line of her jaw and forced her to look up. A muscle tensed at the corner of his mouth as he stared down at the tear-ravaged face. She closed her eyes, and the small spasm flickered again at the corner of his mouth. 'It doesn't make any difference, you know.'

'What doesn't?'

'That your eyes are red and your make-up's ruined. It doesn't make any difference at all.'

Her mouth parted, and her sudden flutter of hands against him came too late. He bent to her lips, determined, refusing to allow evasion, and his hands conveyed their message of desire. Deep within her, Gerda's

142

own senses spelled out their message of warning, even as the force of her own long-pent desire struggled to break its bonds.

As though he sensed that her distress had made her vulnerable to him, he began to caress her more passionately, his mouth demanding and forceful, until all she wanted to do was seek bruised oblivion in his arms. At last he broke the kiss and turned his face against her hair.

His mouth moved in the soft fragrant silkiness, ruffled it where it curled in a smooth sweep from her temple. 'I've wanted to do that for years.'

The words were low spoken, muffled, yet every nuance hammered in her ear. She hadn't imagined them, hadn't imagined the smouldering unspoken awareness sensed every moment she was in contact with him. *Nor had he!* Her heart leapt with response, even as she knew she didn't want to move or speak lest she break the spell. Her lips formed his name soundlessly against the white silk of his shirt before she raised her head to seek confirmation of her own longing in his eyes.

His heavy lashes shadowed his eyes and without speaking he kissed her again, a long sweet kiss that seemed to say everything: it vanquished all resistance and brought her arms round him to capture the beloved silvery head within her interlaced hands. He sighed against her and the pressure of his arms was a sweet agony. Long moments later he stirred.

'Gerda, stay with me. Tonight.'

The warm spinning world stopped, began to chill. She stiffened. 'Stay ... you mean ...?'

'I want you. I've always wanted you.'

The hands locked under her jacket were suddenly unbelievably strong. She tensed, drawing into herself within them. 'I—I can't. Don't ask me.'

'Why not? You want me as much as I want you.'

'No.' Abruptly she twisted free and stumbled away from him. 'That's not true. You——'

'You were just doing that for the fun of it?'

'No, I didn't want you to—to start making love to me. It——' she clenched her hands and opened them in mute expression of her despair, 'it—I didn't mean it that way.'

'It just happened.' His voice was tautly controlled, betraying the simmering anger beneath. 'It always does —just happen. And it's always the man's fault. Never the girl's when she suddenly decides she doesn't mean it at all. Well,' he shot at her, 'it's true, isn't it? You're all the same.'

'Oh no! That's unfair!' She whirled round and faced the scorn in his eyes. 'I didn't say that. Nor did I come here to invite you to start making love to me.'

'No?' His mouth regained its mockery. 'But you *are* an invitation, my dear Gerda. You can't help it, and I'll take a great deal of convincing that you aren't fully aware of it.'

His arrogant power was unassailable. Unable to bear the impact of that steely-dark gaze, she looked away, bitterly conscious of her weakness and the traitorous desire he had roused. For a moment he continued to watch her, as though he sensed the warring emotions she tried to subdue and considered how best to turn them to his own advantage, then he took a step forward.

He said softly, 'Sometimes you almost succeed in convincing me that you've had a change of heart, only for me to find that nothing's changed, and that only makes me want to shatter once and for all that cool innocence you wear so resolutely.'

There was purpose in those slow, deceptively casual steps that brought him within finger-tip distance, and something in the curve of his mouth that told her he was not unaware of his arrogant magnetism for her. He said silkily, 'I could make you, you know, quite easily.'

'Without regard for my wishes?' A crazy defiance made her stand her ground.

'I don't think you know your wishes—regarding me —or you won't admit to them.' With calculated challenge he took hold of the lapels of her jacket and slowly slid it off her shoulders. Despite the warmth of the June evening her skin seemed to chill under the sheer Chinese silk of her blouse, and she had never been so aware of Jordan Black's manhood as at this moment.

He said softly, 'You're too beautiful to fight, my little ice-girl. I'd far rather make love to you.'

He drew the jacket away and dropped it on a low table near by without once taking his gaze from her face, then raised his hands and cupped her head between them. 'You've challenged me too long and too often, Gerda. Now I'm taking that challenge.'

Suddenly a great weariness sapped her spirit. He was too strong to fight any more. What was there to fight any more? Only her own longing and the conflicting loyalties that had brought only pain and disillusion. Let him love her. Perhaps her surrender was the only way in which to sublimate the bitterness he had for her. With a tiny mute gesture of defeat she bowed her head against his shoulder.

His arms closed round her and she did not know if he heard the whispered words that were at once surrender and denial:

'No, Jordan, it was never—that!'

*   *   *

She had first met Jordan Black at a houseboat party near Windsor, not long after she had become friendly with Stuart. He hadn't taken the slightest notice of her, and his greeting, when Stuart made the introductions, had seemed almost disinterested. For quite a while afterwards she had experienced a distinct sense of pique, without really trying to analyse the exact reason for it, and it was not until a couple of months later, during that never-to-be-forgotten first weekend at Green Rigg, that she had at last realised exactly what was the matter with her and why everyone and everything retreated into a nebulous blur when Jordan Black came into her sight.

But by then Stuart was completely infatuated with her. Opportunities of seeing Jordan, except the most casual of meetings, were nil, and she had to face the disquieting knowledge that it was Jordan's attraction all the time which was the true motive behind her continued association with his young brother.

The knowledge tormented her with guilt. Several times she had been tempted to confess to Stuart, make one of those brittle, careless statements which seemed to come so easily to the gay young people in Stuart's set: 'No, it's your brother I fancy, darling,' but such a confession was beyond her, totally opposed to her nature, and besides, she would have died rather than risk her secret being known, last of all to Jordan himself. The days had become torment after that, until the night Stuart asked her to marry him.

His proposal had been typical of his wild attitude to living and life, filled with a boastful, strangely inverted triumph that he should fall victim to her to the extent of being prepared to sacrifice his freedom to marriage. When she had refused him, as gently as she could, he had first been astonished, then unbelieving, and finally

146

angry. Hurt pride had made him say things it was doubtful he would otherwise have said, but they had still hurt, despite this, and revealed more clearly the unstable, selfish side of his nature. At last he had accused her of two-timing him with Blaise Manston, an accusation so unfounded it stung her to bitter denial. Blaise had become to her the patient, unfailing friend that Howard Durrel had been to her mother. She had never once considered Blaise in the light of a possible lover, nor did it ever occur to her to wonder if Blaise ever saw her as anything else than a shy, painfully sensitive girl of eighteen who was taking a little longer than her contemporaries to grow up to awareness of her cool flowering beauty, and on whom fate had bestowed a deep warm vein of generous affection and a selfless sense of duty to those she loved—perhaps too great an unselfishness in one so young.

No, Blaise was someone who was there when she most needed him, for whom she had affection and deep gratitude, and something else that was almost, but not quite love. And it was to Blaise whom she turned such a little while later when fate wove the final strand in the web from which her own compassion would not allow her to break free. In his quiet, undemanding way he had gradually created a haven in which she had found the peace that comes from giving, and knowing that the giving has brought a measure of happiness to another, but she had never been able to forget.

The strange mixture of love and dread she felt for Jordan Black never died; it merely lay dormant where she willed it into the depths of memory. But sometimes an unforeseen happening would spark it back to life; tiny things like seeing a stranger with steely glinting hair and a yellow polo-necked shirt and dark glasses, like coming across a little white jacket with gilt buttons lying forgotten at the back of her wardrobe, bumping into a mutual acquaintance one day in a coffee bar and hearing his name, and once, heartshakingly, his face leaping to her gaze from a newspaper photograph....

But always she had resisted the memories, despising them as disloyalty to Blaise, until his young sister had a whirlwind courtship and marriage. When the couple returned from their honeymoon on Capri there was a brief family reunion down at Blaise's mother's home in Devon. The weather had been glorious that weekend and they had spent most of the time on the beach. It was during that weekend she gained her first full insight into the joy of a relationship between a man and a girl completely and utterly in love with one another. She had been quiet when she and Blaise returned home, and it was then, during the lonely wakeful hours of that night, that she had given way for the first time to longing and the dangerous spell of fantasy.

In imagery she tried to divine the essence of a perfect love, the tenderness and the passion, the shared secrets and the meeting of glances in which intimacy shut out all the rest of the world, the laughter and the teasing and the quiet of content, all that made up the wonder of belonging. And into her vision came a dark shadowy face, and the eyes looked down on her with love and tenderness. His hair was thick and silver-crisp through her fingers, his voice was a caress, and his love was a perfect thing, not ...

* * *

She shivered convulsively and huddled back away from his harshness.

'Why didn't you tell me?'

'Would you have believed me?' Her voice was ragged with bitterness.

'Of course I—— Oh God, how do I know?'

She looked at the outline of his hunched shoulders and felt numb. 'Does it make any difference?' she said wearily.

'Of course it makes a difference!' He got up and paced across the room. 'Of course it makes a difference. I've never pretended to be a saint, but I draw the line at seducing innocents.'

She shivered within the wrap he had thrown at her after those moments of furious renunciation and wondered dully if this were the nadir of all misery. There had to be a way of ending it, but for the moment she was beyond conscious effort. She said hopelessly, 'It doesn't matter.'

He swung round, his face still a dark mask of bitter frustration. 'I still can't believe it.'

'Then don't!' A spasm of anger shook her. 'I've told you, it doesn't matter.'

'But it does!' He came back and sat on the edge of the bed. 'It *does* matter—to me.' He stared at her averted face and the brooding shadows darkened his eyes. 'I thought when you—— You let me carry you in here. You let me believe ... Why? Why, for heaven's sake?'

She could find no answer to the bitter accusation, and he ran his hand over his hair. 'I never dreamed that you—that you're untouched. I——' He shook his head, almost wonderingly, and his voice was quieter. 'What else could I think? Blaise ... your marriage....'

'It was never a real marriage.' She made the admission with difficulty, then her voice sharpened with defensive anger. 'Does that shock you?'

'No, but—— Oh, I don't know what to think.' He

149

fell silent, plainly ill at ease and more disturbed now than she would ever have credited.

'No one ever knew. Not until now,' she said in a low voice. 'You see, Blaise——'

Suddenly he touched her hand. 'You don't have to explain. I——'

She withdrew from a contact she couldn't bear from him at that moment. 'No, I—I think I want to tell someone. It's—I suppose this is my fault. I shouldn't have tried to—let you believe I wanted you to love me all the time, instead of——' She swallowed hard, and his mouth tightened.

'Don't, Gerda.' He reached for his cigarette case and took out two. He lit one and gave it to her. 'Tell me about Blaise—if it'll make it any easier.'

Strangely, she did now want to tell someone, and in a way she couldn't fathom, it had to be this man. She said slowly, 'You once told me you suspected I'd married Blaise out of pity. Well, it's true. I did. I suppose it sounds an impossible arrangement, but it—it wasn't for the reason you really believed,' her mouth trembled, 'it wasn't to escape from marrying Stuart, because I was guilty over what happened to him, or——'

Jordan winced. 'Don't, Gerda,' he repeated, and she knew he was remembering those callous accusations as clearly as she.

'It went back to before that—to the time of my mother's illness,' she went on in a small flat voice. 'The doctor said it was essential that she should not spend the winter in England. He advised a spell in a Swiss clinic, then a long convalescence where it was warm and dry. He made the arrangements and I took a week of my holidays to go over there with her and see her settled down. Blaise was a patient in the same clinic. He'd had one lung removed, but his heart was very badly affected. Because he was English it was natural that we were drawn to him, and he was so kind, reassuring my mother. She was dreadfully nervous. She'd hardly ever been ill in her life before, and she was terrified in case she was going to die. I was frightened in case she was going to fret and make herself worse, but when the time came for me to leave her and return home I wasn't so worried because Blaise was so kind and I knew he would reassure her even more than the doctors could.

'I'd been home about six weeks when I had a letter from her, saying she was feeling so much better and that she was expecting to travel the following week to a health resort near the Tamina Gorge—I can't pronounce the name of the place,' she interjected with a shaky smile, 'but it's a famous spa, and it was while she was there she met Professor Hertz—they got married a few months later and she settled there permanently—he deals in antiques and rare books near the university in Graz, but his home is outside the town and they're wonderfully happy.'

She paused, realising she had digressed. 'In her letter she told me that Blaise was on his way home and that he was coming to see me. He took me out to dinner and we talked about Mother and Switzerland, and his work. He was an artist, mostly illustrative and book jackets, and he was reasonably successful, said he recognised his limitations and had been a great deal happier once he had done so. He was quite a lot older than me. He'd been married, but his wife had died two years previously. When my mother married again I had to decide whether or not to go and live over there. I knew they wanted me, and my stepfather is the kindest and gentlest of men, but I wasn't sure if I wanted to leave England and everything, not for good, and while everybody said, oh yes, I should, Blaise advised me not to if I wasn't sure, and to let my mother settle down to her new marriage for a while. Later, when I went for a long holiday, I knew he was right. My mother and her Professor were completely wrapped in each other. He was doing some mediaeval translations and she was helping him, and she'd become a very fluent linguist in an amazingly short time. I just felt superfluous—she didn't need me to look after her any more. When I came home I met Stuart, and Blaise stood back. I hadn't realised how much I was taking without giving. He was just someone who was always there when I needed him. Then I found out something he'd never told me. That his other lung was affected and there wasn't anything they could do. They'd given him a year at the most.'

Gerda stirred, and Jordan leaned forward to take the cigarette that smouldered unheeded in her hand. His expression was intent, and he prompted: 'And then ...?'

She made a small gesture and looked away, suddenly guarded. 'The rest you know. I—I realised I didn't love Stuart, and then, when it happened, I—I didn't know what to do. I was desperately unhappy, and one night Blaise suddenly asked me if I would marry him. He said he knew he had nothing to offer me, and he would quite understand if I was outraged at his suggestion, but he said if I wouldn't go and make my home with my parents I should think over his suggestion. He knew me so well, you see,' she said carefully, unable to tell Jordan the final confidences that made the picture complete, 'and I knew he would never bring me unhappiness. Suddenly I knew I did want Blaise, and I did love him very much and wanted to make him happy and look after him.'

She took a deep breath. 'We were very happy, and though I used secretly to dread what we knew had to come, we found we could still laugh and be content. There were days when Blaise was ill, terribly ill, but he was so brave I had to be brave too. And—and when the year was past, and he seemed to be getting well for a little while we dared to hope the doctors had been wrong, or a miracle was happening. We had almost another year, and then it all came to an end last year, just before Christmas. We——' her voice was becoming unsteady, 'we were going down to Devon for the holidays, but Blaise wasn't well enough to travel. He—he died in hospital the day before Christmas Eve.'

There was a long silence after she finished speaking. At last Jordan moved and rested his hands on his knees for a moment before he stood up and paced across the room. He said, 'And what were you left with? Security and a few memories?'

He had his back to her, and she could not define exactly the true meaning behind his words. She said quietly: 'No, but I learned to know someone who was a great person. There was never any pretence about our marriage. I gave him companionship and affection which I hope helped to make the pitifully short time left to him happier than it might otherwise have been, and he gave me peace and understanding when I most needed it. I have no regrets about Blaise and I was proud to be his wife.'

Jordan turned, and his mouth was compressed, as though he was on the point of saying something and changed his mind. Instead, he said flatly: 'Blaise might have lingered on for years. Would you still have felt the same about your marriage?'

'Yes!' The affirmative was fiercely whispered, but despite her vehemence she was dangerously near breaking point. The numbness was dissolving and reality was crowding back fast. She had to escape.

But he appeared not to heed her uncertainty, nor to realise that she craved to be left alone to repair dishevelment after the fiasco of her despairing submission. Abruptly he came back, and for the first time she saw uncertainty, remorse, and something very like tenderness in his face. He said awkwardly:

'This all makes a difference—you do understand? I would never have behaved as I did, if I'd known what you've just told me.'

Now, when she least expected it, he suddenly put his arms round her, in an attempt at a rough, shamed kind of comfort. 'I'm not trying to make excuses, but you've got to believe that.'

But Jordan had forgotten a woman's pride and its power to subdue all other emotions, even the virtue of forgiveness. At the moment Jordan's touch was the last thing in the world she wanted. It was too potent, and it was unbearable. She pulled away. 'Yes, I told you ... It doesn't matter.'

Her movement of repudiation was harsh. Jordan's arms fell from her and he straightened. His mouth was bitter. He said flatly: 'Yes, I suppose whichever way you look at it I'm wrong.'

She pushed her hair out of her eyes and groped for her shoes. 'Please ...' she said wearily, 'I just want to forget it. I'm *not* blaming you.'

'No, but your eyes are.'

She smoothed her hair with resigned, dogged movements, as though she had not heard him, and he gave a sharp exclamation.

'All right!' He lifted his hands, then let them drop back to his sides. 'So I was wrong about you—in one way, at least. And I discovered that interesting fact in time. For which you should thank me.' His mouth twisted sardonically. 'But no woman's crazy logic would ever recognise that. If I'd seduced you, you'd have retreated into tragic reproach. But because I didn't I insulted you by failing to. Is that it?' he said bitterly.

Oh no! Gerda's face crumpled and blind impassioned anger possessed her. She was too distraught to perceive that Jordan had taken refuge in the bluster of shame and frustration, she saw only the final cruel destruction of her illusions. An innocent without experience! A *fool*!

Heedless now of anguish blinding her, or his attempts to reason with her and persuade her to let him drive her home, she rushed out into the night to seek the blessed friendly anonymity of darkness.

CHAPTER VIII

DURING that miserable weekend Gerda swung wildly between bitter unreasoning hatred of all men—Jordan Black in particular—and an equally unreasoning fever of self-contempt. She lost sight of her original desperate motive in seeking to influence Jordan's action and could agonise only over its result. Now, she had not only failed to persuade him to reconsider his decision, but she had also forfeited what little respect he might still have held for her, to say nothing of her own self-respect.

She was wan and wretched in spirit when she set off for the hospital on the Sunday. But for her promise and for the fact that Howard would be transferred to the convalescent home the following day she would have cried off the visit; in her present mood and with her bad tidings, she was no fit visitor for a sick man. However, he was looking so well and cheerful when she found him sitting outside on the visitors' terrace that a momentary lightening pervaded her spirit, only to give way to a fresh misgiving as she realised that he was still in ignorance of the events at Charingfolds.

He smiled, his eyes crinkled against the bright sunshine, and held out his hand when he saw her approaching.

'Isn't it a beautiful day?' he said when she sat down at his side.

Gerda had not noticed, if the skies had fallen it was doubtful if it would have registered with her, but she tried to smile brightly and agreed.

'If it stays like this I shall enjoy my convalescence, I shall walk and laze in the sun, and perhaps indulge in a gentle game of bowls. Then I shall know I'm hovering on the brink of old age,' he added wryly.

'You're not in the least old,' she said firmly, 'nor is playing bowls a sign of it. It's having quite a revival in popularity.'

'Is it?' Howard's smile became vague, then faded altogether. 'Is something the matter, my dear? You look troubled.'

'No, there's nothing the matter.' She forced herself to sound bright. 'I'm fine.'

'Are you? You don't look it. Can I help?'

'No—it's nothing,' she persisted, 'except that ...' She stopped, knowing that she must tell him and dismayed at his perception. She had wanted to tell him gently, not alarm him, not betray her own concern.

'Except what?' He frowned. 'Gerda, are you worrying about me and the firm? That contract business? Because I——'

'Yes—oh, I didn't want to worry you. I had hoped to be able to tell you that ...' Suddenly she was pouring out her confession of failure, in short broken phrases, totally unlike her usual calm concise way of talking to him. '... I know it's business, but it was such a cold letter, and—and so I suddenly decided to go and see him. I asked Hugh Merrick not to tell you—until I'd seen Jordan Black—and then I didn't get round to ringing him until last night and he was out, so he doesn't know what happened. But it was hopeless. I—I did see Jordan Black, but he—he wouldn't change his mind. I—I was a fool to think he would take any notice of me. But I'd hoped....' She stopped, and her mouth quivered. 'I'm afraid I just made things worse instead of——'

'And this is what is distressing you so much?' Howard interrupted.

She nodded, too concerned with her own fear of the effect this was having on her employer to notice that he did not seem completely dismayed.

He said slowly, 'I'm beginning to wonder if you took a certain light-hearted remark of mine too literally.' A flash of puzzlement widened her eyes and he gave a slight smile. 'When I suggested that you'd make a most charming ambassadress—remember? I hope you didn't take my remarks too seriously and . . .' he hesitated, his glance shrewd, 'allow yourself to become—shall I say? —personally involved with Black?'

Her heart lurched. With an effort she controlled her voice. 'I—I don't know if I ever told you . . . I knew his younger brother, some years ago, quite well. So in a way there was a personal element involved. But it didn't make any difference.'

'No, I don't suppose it would. It's always a mistake to allow personal elements to enter into business matters. I think it has caused more enemies to be made and more friendships to be broken than anything else.' He fell silent, considering her somewhat guarded divulgence, then added thoughtfully, 'I just wondered. It's so unlike you to get into a flap like this. But you mustn't let it concern you. I appreciate your loyalty, my dear—you know I don't have to tell you that—but I shall be very angry if I find you're allowing my worries to upset you.

'Well,' with a small inclination of his head he appeared to dismiss the matter, 'now I shall tell you *my* news! Oh, yes, I'm not completely divorced from the world—even in here. As you haven't been in contact with Merrick since Friday you won't know that he came along to see me yesterday. In fact, I had quite a hectic day yesterday, what with one thing and another. However, I'm afraid he told me everything, including your gallant little effort to nail Black.' Howard gave her a quick glance in which sympathy flashed and pursed his mouth. 'I didn't intend to tell you I'd heard about that little business, but as you've told me yourself, Merrick had to see me in any case. He couldn't let things slide any longer. We had a long discussion and I told him my decision. He wasn't very happy about it, but I think he realises it is the only one I can make.'

She tensed. Suddenly she had a presentiment of something disturbing about to be imparted. Howard seemed to be choosing his words carefully and as he began she knew her impression was not unfounded.

He leaned back and looked at the peaceful sunlit grounds, and said slowly: 'I've been doing a lot of thinking during these last few days, and I've faced something I wouldn't face before this illness. I'm losing my grip, so I'm going to pull out.

'Yes,' he met her startled gaze, 'out of Charingfolds. I'm going to retire. I'll sell my town house and make the little place in Devon my permanent home—you'll have to come for a holiday—and lead a blissfully simple life.'

She could still only gaze at him. This was the last thing she had expected to hear. Howard! Giving up! She shook her head wonderingly. 'I can't believe it. I know I—and others—have often urged you to let up a bit—you do drive yourself hard—but retiring! What will you do with yourself all day?'

'Walk, and fish, and grow roses. Maybe write that book I've always wanted to write. I shall get out of the treadmill at last, and I shall be very happy.'

'Yes,' she sighed. 'You deserve it. And I shall hold you to that promise.'

'I hope you will, because I'm quite aware that I'll miss the dear old rat race. There'll be times when I'll get restless, maybe even regret my decision, but they'll get less frequent and I shall have the knowledge that my decision was the right one, not only for myself but for my colleagues and Charingfolds.'

'I can't imagine what it'll be like without you,' she said at last, still not able to grasp at it all. 'It's going to be awful.'

'You're just being very kind and sentimental.' He shook his head. 'In a couple of months I'll just be a memory in the back of a filing cabinet—if that. And if Merrick grabs you for his P.S.—which he'll do for certain—you'll soon settle down again. You'll be all right with him.'

'Yes.' She sighed and her eyes held doubt. 'It isn't that....' Suddenly she wondered who would merge from the juggle for power and take Howard's place. Then she remembered something else and a stab of alarm brought her head up sharply. What had Jordan said? He was considering a bid for Charingfolds!

She met Howard's enquiring glance and bit back the words she had nearly blurted out. Jordan had merely intimated that he was *considering* it. He could change his mind. He could have made a rare unguarded confidence which might prove to be based on a mere notion he was contemplating, not one already decided. Would it be wise to repeat his words?

While she wavered Howard said abruptly: 'Anyway, we'll all know our fate after tomorrow's meeting. I'll be along by ten-thirty and going down by car to Hampshire after lunch. By the way,' he stood up and his manner was quite relaxed, 'will you book my usual table for me, for twelve-thirty?'

'Yes, of course. Is there anything else?' she asked

automatically.

'I don't think so—except to take that worried look off your face.' He patted her shoulder and began to stroll slowly back towards the ward entrance. 'It's all going to be all right.'

But was it?

The atmosphere was tense and hushed over the office the following morning. The staff looked wary and uncertain, and no one had a great deal to say. Despite the bright sunshine the boardroom felt chill and unfriendly, and even the flowers which Elizabeth had hastily arranged on the window sill could not soften the hardness of the long polished table and the clinically gleaming row of glasses and ashtrays.

Howard was the last to arrive, a minute or two late, so Gerda had no opportunity of speaking to him, except for an exchange of good mornings before she took her unobtrusive place at one side and opened a neat folder in readiness for any notes she might have to make.

It was a dour meeting and an unusually quiet one, and the air of depression had subdued even Merrick's bluff noisiness. It was more a note of sadness, subtly different, and she wondered if the news of Howard's decision had been leaked out beforehand. She decided it must have been, for there was little genuine surprise when he made the announcement.

Gerda felt her throat constrict during the small silence that followed. She could not help the sad reflection that this was the last time Howard Durrel would preside over a meeting in this room. Someone else would be sitting there, someone with a set of totally different little mannerisms from the ones she knew so well. He was leaning forward now, clearing his throat and pausing as he always did before he emphasised a point. No, it would never be the same again.... Then she tensed, heard him speaking, and knew that the emotions surging through her were not surprise or shock but dismay and a strange sense of fatalism, as though she should have known all along.

Quietly, in unemotional tones, Howard outlined his proposals and Jordan Black's bid for a working directorship.

There were only two dissenting voices in the vote.

It was the beginning of the end for Charingfolds. It meant that it was inevitable that Wentford would eventually become the holding company. Basically Charingfolds would appear the same, but their policies would be controlled by Wentford, gradually the new innovations would creep in, new faces would appear and old ones fade. But to Gerda it meant only two things: that Jordan Black would become the usurper of Howard's place, and that her own days with the firm must end. Jordan Black was the last man she could bear to acknowledge as the man in authority.

But why hadn't Howard told her? He must have been in touch with Jordan. Must have known. Automatically she made her notes, was dimly aware of a discussion of necessary amendments to the company's articles of association, and heard the door open.

She closed her folder and looked up, and saw Jordan Black coming into the room.

The meeting had broken up, but she remained sitting there, suddenly numbed. She saw Howard go to meet him. Jordan offered his hand and Howard clasped it, smiling. The gap of silence caused by his entrance filled again with the rumble of voices as Howard made introductions. The men moved around, informal and less strained now, and the long polished table suddenly looked deserted, forlorn under a clutter of papers, someone's pen, a smouldering cigarette on the lip of an ashtray, and the faint blue pall of smoke above.

Gerda stood up, her composure shattered, and held the folder pressed tight to her as Jordan's glance found her. Only the slightest flicker of his brow betrayed recognition, then he returned his attention to something Hugh Merrick was saying.

Elizabeth came into the room and made straight towards her, saying something, but Gerda did not hear. She was conscious only of watching Howard pick up his briefcase and shake hands briefly with his fellow directors. There were no lingering farewells. He smiled at Jordan Black and the two men walked out together without a backward glance at her or anyone.

The coldness of irony closed round her heart, and she felt as though she had been betrayed. What a stupid sentimental fool she'd been! What a waste of all her heartache....

      *   *   *

The rest of that day was agony. She found it impossible to concentrate on the letters that had to be done, and at the finish Merrick lost patience, controlling his never very certain temper with difficulty.

'For God's sake, girl! I didn't say "with reference to the proposed changes in policy and the threat of redundancy ..." I said: "with reference to the threatened redundancy caused by re-organisation of our costing department". Read it back again.'

'I'm sorry,' she faltered. 'Could you go back to "programming", please? I'm lost.'

'Lost!' Merrick raised despairing eyes and started again.

'You'll have to do better than this, my girl,' he said later that afternoon. 'Especially when the new régime gets going.'

His tone was not really unkind, but it started the ache all over again. 'I don't think I want to stay with the new régime,' she said flatly.

'So that's it.' Merrick pursed his mouth. 'I might have known. It won't make much difference to you. Things always shake down.'

She was silent, and the thought was taking substance. For her peace of mind a change was indicated; complete break, perhaps even in another part of the country. It was the only way.

'If you're worrying about Black you needn't. It'll be hell around the joint when he does blow in—it always is with the whizz kid types—but it won't be often. The occasional meeting. This is only one of his sidelines. If we see him more than a dozen times in the year I'll be very surprised.'

She flinched from Merrick's astute shot in the dark— if shot in the dark it was—regarding her lapse from efficiency, but she was not consoled by his comfortable surmise.

At home that evening she looked round the flat with mournful eyes. Could she bear to break up the home she and Blaise had made? It had taken so long to adjust to the loneliness he had left. What would it be like in a strange town somewhere where she knew no one at all? She could find a different job; she didn't have to find a new home as well. But somehow she couldn't think straight, and still the subconscious idea of making a complete break nagged at her, taunting her to face the truth; that the only way to peace of mind was to remove herself where she would never see or hear of Jordan Black again.

He was like a raw aching wound inside her, like a thorn driven deep that she longed to pluck out but did not dare to probe. How was she going to forget him and forget her own helpless emotion? For a wild moment she wished that she possessed the courage and the ability to play the temptress, Instinct told her that Jordan would not have been entirely proof against that power. But would it have made any difference to the anguish she was suffering now? Did the sharing of the climax of physical desire magically resolve the antagonism between the two people concerned? Make a bond between them that helped them to accept their conflicting differences? In those moments of despairing decision when Jordan had demanded her surrender she had believed that it might be so, that in the ultimate surrender to him she might sublimate this bitter enchantment and free herself from him for ever.

But did it work out that way?

A dreadful apathy possessed her as the week wore on. She was almost afraid to enter the office each day lest Jordan Black should suddenly confront her, or that she should pick up the phone and hear his voice. But he did not appear, and the three phone calls he did make were taken by Merrick. She almost began to relax as the week drew to its close and believe that Merrick had been correct in his assumption. They would not see him very often. She did not have to rush over this decision that was increasingly difficult to make. Then, on the Friday, when they were slowing up, looking forward to the freedom of the weekend, Jordan Black arrived.

He wasted no time on polite preliminaries. With a curt request to Merrick for the provision of an escort, he set off on an exhaustive tour of Charingfolds.

To Gerda's relief she was spared this. Young Mr

Taylor did the escorting, with a hastily summoned and apprehensive young secretary from the accounts department. She returned with a crammed notebook and the hope that it would be somebody else's turn next time, and Jordan retained his miniature recorder from which his report would be transcribed.

Elizabeth hurried in with a tray of coffee, only to be summoned to the phone, and Gerda was forced to act as hostess. She found she was silently praying that no malign fate would erupt some dire emergency to claim Hugh Merrick and young Mr Taylor, leaving her alone at the mercy of Jordan Black.

She had no option but to pour out three cups of coffee and hand them round. Inwardly she was trembling, afraid of the smallest of accidental contacts as she took the coffee to him, and, as she had always done when Howard had visiting executives, ensured that the cigarette box, desk lighter, and ashtray were within convenient reach. Jordan sat there calmly, immaculate as always in dark city clothes. He always appeared to have just stepped out after shaving and changing, and there was about him an almost tangible air of taut strength and controlled vitality as he watched her with a cool scrutiny she found intensely unnerving.

Not moving, he murmured 'Thank you' in his clipped tones, and there was only the curtest suggestion of a smile at the corners of his mouth.

It was as though she were a stranger, and yet in those hard, enigmatic eyes there was a recognition that instantly fired the smouldering memories of the hours in the house at Innescourt Mews. She turned away abruptly, unable to make even an impersonal response. Her face felt as though fiery waves of heat radiated from it and it cost her some effort to resist pressing her icy hands against her cheeks to mask the betraying

166

carlet. Thankful that she could now slip away, she made for the door, only to be checked by Merrick's voice.

He asked her to get out two copies of the contract which had led to the renewal of all her heartbreak, then said genially: 'Aren't you having your coffee, girl?'

This was the one time when she would have blessed a complete formality. But it was not to be. Silently she sorted out the two copies of the contract, placing one at Merrick's hand, then laying the other one in front of Jordan Black. Now she no longer cared whether he signed it or not.

He looked up and made a gesture of negotiation. 'I have a copy—remember?' He opened his briefcase and drew out the copy with a complete absence of fumbling.

She was forced to reach over and take the other copy back, and felt certain he had made the unnecessary insistence to cause her discomfiture. Wishing she could escape but not daring to risk being recalled again if she did so, she poured herself a cup of coffee and took it to her own desk near the window, where she sat down carefully at an angle which would keep her out of the direct range of his vision.

Sitting stiffly, she got out a folder and opened it, making a pretence of work, while behind her Jordan Black signed the fateful contract with a brisk carelessness that was a mockery. She heard Merrick say something, and Jordan laugh, and once again the sense of betrayal filled her with anguish. He could afford to laugh. He was merely taking with one hand what he gave with the other. First Van-Lorn; now Charingfolds. Both in the net. Howard had bowed out without regret, exactly as Jordan had predicted. All along the line he had known exactly what he was doing, and while he knew he had played with her, testing her loyalty even as he accused her of owning none. Well, she had learned her lesson, she thought bitterly. This was the end of personal involvements and loyalty in future. Wherever she went she was going to make sure it was amid strangers, and she would do her work efficiently but impersonally, and nothing more. And one day she would be able to forget....

'Is this where you usually work?'

The soft smoothness of charcoal-dark barathea brushed her arm. She said, 'Yes,' without looking up or moving.

'You should always work with the light falling over your shoulder—the left one, preferably, I'm told—never facing you.'

He moved round behind her, to stand at her other side, and rested his hands on the desk top. The nails were pale and well shaped, there were dark hairs on his wrists, and the second hand of a Rolex automatic ticked steadily round the luminous dial. He slid his hand across the desk top. 'This surface is too reflective to light. You'd work better with a matt surface and your desk re-sited to the left here.'

'I've worked quite comfortably and efficiently here for nearly seven months.'

The supple fingers flexed and curled under, and a white cuff partly obscured the Rolex. 'I wasn't questioning your efficiency. Few people realise how incorrect working positions cause strain until they make the adjustments to correct their own particular misalignment. Agreement on the resultant benefit is always enthusiastic,' he said dryly.

She took a deep breath. 'Thank you for your advice, Mr Black. I appreciate it, but it isn't necessary.' The hands fell away and the desk top looked curiously blank. She stared steadily in front of her. 'You see, I won't be working here much longer.'

There was a brief hesitation, then the sensing of him drawing back. He said coolly, 'The principle applies wherever you happen to be working. By the way, Stuart is getting married tomorrow.'

He did not wait for any response, and there was only Merrick walking through the doorway when at last she turned her head.

A cloud passed over the sun as she watched Jordan walk to his car. The steely hair went duller in the overcast light, and the chill seemed to penetrate the warm office. The car eased back out of the parking place, and somehow there was a curious sense of finality in the way it diminished and disappeared from her sight.

Elizabeth had to speak twice when she came into the room before Gerda came out of her apathy, then she had to ask the older woman to repeat her remark.

'I said,' Elizabeth enunciated distinctly, 'that it looks like fireworks and lightning ahead—the lightning's struck already in the general office.'

'How?' said Gerda dully.

'Well,' Elizabeth waved her hands, 'our latest blue-eyed baby dolly is obviously going to be useless for the rest of the day. She's still got her head stuck out of the window—with an expression very much like the one *you're* wearing at the moment, my girl. Actually, I think she's planning to stay there until Jordan Black comes into sight again down that drive.'

'Really?'

'Yes, really,' Elizabeth nodded sagely. 'I suppose he's got what it takes to turn a fly-away head that's dying to be turned—if you're the type that prefers danger to a shy pass in the canteen. Thank goodness I'm immune now.'

You're lucky! Gerda thought bitterly. Aloud, she said, 'He'll soon cure them of *that*!

'Ho ho! Like that, is it?' Elizabeth sniffed comically and slid off the corner of Gerda's desk. She looked out of the window, then turned away with a sigh of reluctance. 'Oh, well, back to the grind. I suppose life does go on.'

The echo of Elizabeth's wry observation stayed with Gerda the rest of that day. At the present her own life felt more like a limbo to be existed through, one beyond which she was incapable of seeing how she was going to reform it into a bearable future. Somehow she had to pull herself together and make plans for a fresh start; she couldn't go on like this, and she couldn't bear to stay at Charingfolds. Not now. But where? And what?

And Stuart was getting married. It would be Rachel, of course. It had to be. The clipped statement was typical of Jordan, giving no indication of his attitude. Had he changed his mind, softened enough to give his blessing? It seemed doubtful. Her own experience of Jordan Black told her that he neither changed his mind, nor relented. Certainly the last thing he did was soften.

She thought dully that she should phone Stuart, congratulate him and wish them both happiness, but such was her state of dejection that she could not bring herself to make the effort, until a particularly harrowing documentary began on the TV and despising herself for her squeamishness she switched it off and went to the phone. Why couldn't she be ashamed of giving in to heartbreak when there was so much appalling misery in other people's lives?

At first she did not recognise the responding voice at the other end, until Leon introduced himself and asked her to wait a moment. There seemed to be a great deal of noise in the background, a blare of music and a mingling of voices. Of course, there would be a celebration going on ... then Stuart's voice sounded, lively and surprised.

'Yes, it's true. We're having the celebration first—we're off on the noon flight tomorrow. Rachel's going to her doom and I'm going to the slaughter—if I don't get cold feet again. Did Jordan tell you? I told him to bring you down tonight if you weren't doing anything special, but he said not to bank on it as he expected to be tied up himself. I say, do you want to speak to Rachel? She's around somewhere. I had—*Will somebody turn that damned thing down?* I can't hear myself speak—are you still there?'

'Yes,' she said faintly. Stuart sounded slightly drunk and judging by the hilarity in the background it was a hectic celebration. She said quickly, 'I won't keep you from your party—I just wanted to wish you both happiness and——'

'Sure, sure. Where has she got to? I'm sure she'd want to—she told me she'd had a heart-to-heart with you—I guessed that was why I hadn't heard from you—but she knows now that she needn't be jealous of you—I made my own confession to my dear little bride-to-be last night. It's really a bit of a giggle when you look back, isn't it? All that conspiracy. Rachel was quite shaken—I almost wished I hadn't told her—she tore strips off me. But after all, what else could I do at the time? You were the only one who understood, and after all, it's over and done with, and apart from Jordan who's going to remember it now? I mean, it didn't hurt you, did it?'

He paused, but it wasn't really to wait for the negative assent he took for granted. Then, as though struck by a brilliant idea, he said suddenly: 'I say, why don't you come down tomorrow and see us off? It's just a quiet affair—us and Jordan and Leon—he's got to come with us, of course—but we could have a farewell drink for old times' sake.'

'No!' her voice was breaking. 'I—I can't. I—I'm going away, for the weekend. But thanks all the same. I—I just wanted to wish you happiness and—and I'll be praying for your—for the day you walk again to be very soon. Goodbye, and—good luck.'

Before he could respond she put the receiver down and raised shaking hands to her face. Just like that. Over and done with now ... *it never really hurt her*..... She sank into a chair and suddenly knew she had to get away, anywhere, this weekend. Almost feverishly, as though the purpose was a lifeline, she hunted frantically for a gazetteer. Where could she go? Not the sea? Not the southern countryside, somewhere where she'd never been....

By noon the following day she was wandering through the busy streets of Oxford, a slender, remote-eyed girl who looked curiously detached from the weekend shoppers and visitors, and a little while later she was out in the quiet summer gold and green of the countryside, booking in at a beautful old hotel set among velvet lawns and woodland through which a silvery stream lapped placidly and made a strangely peaceful music.

She stayed there till the Sunday evening, putting off her return until the latest possible train, not caring that it would be midnight or after when she finally let herself back into the lonely flat. She did not know how often the phone had shrilled its vain summons, or of the carillon of the door chimes echoing through the empty rooms. And so almost forty-eight hours elapsed before she heard the dreadful news.

Howard Durrel was dead.

The tired heart had given up, peacefully in his sleep, during the early hours of the Saturday morning. It seemed unbelievable; but it was true.

When the first numbing shock dissolved and tragic reality prevailed she made no effort to constrain her grief. She wept because death was so final and so indifferent of mortal hopes, and she wept because it reduced her own troubles to puny proportions but did not lessen their heartbreak.

CHAPTER IX

It was all over; there was nothing left to do but snap the locks on her case and wait for the taxi. In a few short hours she would be in Vienna, but the thought evoked no stir of excitement. It was people, not places, who made joy and sorrow.

She sat on the arm of the chair by the window and rested her arm along the sill. Her eyes were heavy and listless with the resignation that comes when emotion has drained all vitality and the spirit has accepted defeat. But the sorrow and the vain regrets still haunted her, and she knew it would be a long time before the memories of the last few days would fade. If only they were not so inextricably bound up with the last sharply etched impression of Jordan Black's tall figure standing with bowed head in the garden of remembrance. He had looked at her only once, a cold, remote stranger's glance, before he left silently in the company of a man she did not know. He had made his formal token tribute in respect to Howard Durrel and she had wondered bitterly how much true feeling existed beneath that cold invulnerable façade.

She got up restlessly, glancing at her watch, and tried to force her thoughts to the journey ahead. Because of her absence over the weekend her delay in cabling the tragic news to her mother had been too long. By the time her mother returned from visiting a friend it had been too late to arrange a last tribute to the man who had loved her so unselfishly all those years. She had telephoned Gerda that evening, deeply distressed, and suddenly it was all arranged that Gerda should fly out as soon as she could make the arrangements to do so.

Merrick had been gruff and understanding. He had just said: 'Go, you need a break,' and somehow the tacit understanding had been there unspoken. She wouldn't be coming back.

It was strange, she thought sadly, how life divided itself up into a series of small isolated compartments. Childhood, clearly defined into school and home, its ending unforgettably marked by the loss of her father, then the first job, the tentative discoveries of adulthood, and the first major crisis life sent to test her, before the closing of the door on that part of her life. Then Blaise, another beginning, and now ... Perhaps her mother was right; perhaps it was time she went home. But where was home?

She began a third check of her bag; passport, ticket, currency, silver in her pocket ready to pay the taxi-man ... suddenly she knew a desperate impatience to be gone, and when the chimes rang through the silent flat she paused to gather up everything and take a final look round before she went to the door.

The mental image of a laconic, impersonal cab-driver was too fixed in her mind as her strap-weighted wrist coped with the resistance of the Yale latch and drew the door inward. She blundered a little with the case, and the prepared image still hovered above the focus of her vision as she backed to allow the door to clear her burden.

A hand reached out. 'You can put that down again.'

The impact of reality was so shattering her grip relaxed and the case almost slid from her suddenly nerveless fingers.

Jordan Black took it from her and walked calmly into the flat. He turned and closed the door, and then faced her. 'You'd better sit down. I seem to have given you a shock.'

'I—I——' Her voice didn't seem to want to obey her. It wanted to stick in her throat and stay there. 'But I can't—I'm going away. I'm going to Austria.' Suddenly the constriction freed itself and the words wanted to come tumbling out, a defence. 'I'm going to stay with my mother, and the taxi'll be here any moment. My plane goes at——'

'I know.' He unlooped the handbag and travelling bag from her wrist and dropped them by the case. 'If you're lucky you'll still make your flight. If not it'll be the next one. Don't worry, I'll do the necessary.'

'But you can't!' His implacable command unnerved her and she took a step forward. 'I'll miss the plane, and my mother——'

'I said I'll fix it. Gerda, there are things I have to say, and if they aren't said now they never will be. So sit down and don't argue.'

She backed towards the settee, then started forward again as the chimes sounded. But he barred her way, opening the door and with swift sleight-of-hand appeasing the taxi-driver even as he dismissed the man. She said despairingly: 'That was my taxi. I'll——'

'I heard you the first time. Where do you keep the bottle for guests? Or is the place stripped of everything?'

'In that cupboard—over there.' She sat down weakly and pressed her trembling knees together. 'I don't understand. What do you want? Haven't you—— Why have you come here and—and——' Her voice failed her again and she watched him sort out the half bottle of Martini and the forgotten bottle of ginger cordial left from Christmas.

He grinned and pushed it back, then poured Martini into a wine glass. He came to her and put it into her hand. She stared at him. 'But I don't want a drink! I——'

'Maybe not, but you need one.' Abruptly he sat down at her side and twisted to face her. He started to speak, then abruptly checked, his mouth tightening as he looked at her frightened eyes and saw the shadows like bruised violet petals under the dark lashes. 'Don't look at me like that. As though I ... Why didn't you tell me the truth years ago? Why did you let me believe it so long? Letting me...'

Still she stared at him, and he said explosively, 'I could kill somebody. I could—— Oh, God! How hideously wrong I've been. All this time. And you stayed silent because of a crazy child and a selfish young cub who would let an innocent girl suffer because of his pride and his stupidity. Don't you see? I couldn't let you go away without trying to put things right?' He was speaking more quickly now, as though he couldn't contain the force of the anger he wanted to expend. 'I tried to find you at the weekend. I phoned on Saturday, several times, drove over on Sunday, but you weren't here. Then I saw you at the funeral and I knew it wasn't the right time. I had to give you breathing space. You couldn't take any more. I—I was beginning to glimpse what you must have gone through. Then I heard this morning at Charingfolds that you were going away, and I knew I couldn't let it wait until you came back—if you came back.' He paused. 'Yes, I know it all—enough—and I don't know what to say, except that I'm sorry.'

His words seemed to be coming from a tremendous distance away, and her own words of response felt like a whisper. He said heavily, 'Yes, I know now that you weren't in that car with Stuart. And I know why.'

'Did—did Stuart tell you?'

'No. Rachel told me.'

'Rachel!' Gerda's head came up sharply. 'But when did she—she wasn't supposed——'

'No. She told me just before the wedding. She hadn't known your part in it until Stuart told her. Then she was so aghast she felt she had to tell me.' Jordan took a deep breath. 'There's still a lot I can't fill in. Why it happened in the first place, and why it was necessary to deceive me. Why Stuart had to say it was you. Why you let him lie to me.'

She sighed and looked down at her hands. Now that the burden of misplaced guilt had been lifted she was aware of sudden lightness and a strange indifference. Perhaps the shock of Howard's death made her see the whole thing as a diminished contrast of anguish, perhaps she had reached the stage where even hurt must lose its power, but now she was conscious of a reluctance to go back over the hurt again. It was sufficient that he knew the truth.

He said, 'I know Rachel was driving the car. That she was only fifteen, and had no licence, and that she panicked. I can understand. I can imagine her father's reaction, and the appalling outcry there would have been if the police had got wind of it. But why the devil did Stuart ever let her drive the car in the first place? He knew she was under age, couldn't have a licence, and the only driving she had done was on her father's estate. He must have been insane.'

'He'd been to a party with her. The road was very quiet and she'd begged him to let her try the car,' Gerda said in a low voice. 'Rachel was crazy about him, even then when she was only fifteen. She haunted him —she was very young and she was spoilt, I suppose. You know that Sir Hubert married late in his life and

Rachel was his only child. He doted on her, and used to laugh at her wild escapades when she was a child, so how could he expect her to change like magic? But Stuart never gave her any encouragement. He wasn't having an affair with her, or anything like that—he was more amused by her than anything else.'

'Any female's admiration would amuse Stuart—as long as she was young and attractive enough,' Jordan said grimly. 'But I still don't fathom why he did it.'

'I don't suppose he knew himself,' she said sadly.

'I mean his deliberate hiding of the truth from me.'

'He was frightened, and he was very badly injured,' she reminded him quietly.

'Yes, but it was still wrong.' The taut lines of Jordan's mouth did not relent, and Gerda sighed.

If only Jordan would forget it now that it was all over. Of what use were all these recriminations? If she could forgive Stuart his deception, after suffering Jordan's censure, why couldn't Jordan himself forget his stubborn pride and hurt because his brother had lied to him? She took a deep breath and turned away, aware still of the impulse to defend Stuart. Whatever his sins had been he had paid for them a thousand-fold.

'He wanted to protect Rachel,' she said wearily, 'and he was dazed that night in hospital. He didn't know what he was saying.'

'He knew perfectly well,' Jordan said flatly. 'The first thing he said to me was "Where is she? Is she all right?" and he was scared stiff. This was the first we'd heard of anyone else being involved. We thought he'd been driving alone. But when I asked him who he meant he'd begun to remember properly and he pretended he was confused, and that he'd been alone. It was at this point that I got called out to speak to the doctor and also the police, and I heard this motorist's statement about a girl running away. Of course it had been dark, and the witness wasn't positive she'd come from the wrecked car. When I got back to Stuart I told him he had to tell us, if he'd had a girl passenger we had to know, in case she was wandering around in shock somewhere. He got frightened again, and admitted it, and naturally you were the first person who came to mind. When I asked him direct, he just turned his face away and said who else would he be with. He was going to marry you, wasn't he?' Jordan stopped and gestured despairingly. 'What else could I believe? What else could I do but find you and bring you along? Then *you* confirmed it all. Why?'

'I don't know,' she said helplessly. 'I suppose I felt guilty. You see, I don't know if Stuart told you, but he proposed to me a week before it happened, and he took it very badly when I refused him. But I—I just didn't love him enough, and I knew he was just infatuated with me—the fact that he still saw his other girls, and—and that I——' She stopped, and licked dry lips. 'But that doesn't come into it. When you came to seek me that night I'd never been out. Blaise had arrived only about half an hour before you arrived. If things had been different, if we'd been out, Stuart couldn't have made you believe that ...' Again she hesitated, and Jordan came back to sit at her side and stare at her with worry shadowing his eyes.

'If I hadn't been so frantic I might have realised that your shock was genuine,' he said slowly. 'But I'd got the idea fixed that it was you and you'd run away. Your white face looked like guilt, and then when you started reassuring Blaise and telling him not to worry but you'd have to go with me to see Stuart, I was convinced then. I thought you were trying to hide it from him as well.'

'I didn't want to worry him. That was partly why I agreed to go with you straight away, but when you started talking about this witness who was supposed to have seen me running away—in white——'

'And you were wearing white that night,' he interrupted grimly.

She nodded. 'I began to feel frightened, and then when I saw Stuart I felt so sorry I wanted to cry. He looked so white and——' she gestured mutely, the distress of three years ago suddenly as vivid and real as at the time. 'Do you remember he took hold of my hand and asked you to go away? And you didn't want to, but you did, and then he told me about Rachel. He was terrified. He didn't know what had happened to her, and all he could think about was what would happen if the police found out about her. He begged me to go and find her, see if she was unhurt, and tell her to keep quiet and he would swear he'd never even seen her that night. He whispered that there'd be hell to pay if her father ever got to know about it, or if you ever got to know. Then he told me about this motorist seeing her, and he said he'd had to let Jordan—let you think he'd been with me.'

Beside her, he gave an exclamation of anger, and she spread her hands in a gesture of mute appeal. 'I had to. He looked at me so helplessly, and he was so desperately ill, and then he said it was all his fault, he'd let Rachel drive, and she might have been killed, and he wished he'd been killed himself, and I just couldn't leave him to face it all alone. So I—I let you believe it was me, that I'd run to get help, and the phone in the box was out of order, and when I got back they'd taken Stuart to hospital. It was exactly what had happened to

181

Rachel. I phoned her later, after you'd taken me home and—and——' She faltered, the memory of that scene in the car too painful to dwell on. 'I did as he asked —told her to keep quiet and never tell a soul. I didn't tell her we'd let you think it was me. She was terrified enough as it was.'

'And then Stuart begged me to get it hushed up and swear that he was alone,' Jordan said grimly. 'Naturally I thought he wanted to protect you, and I didn't think it was worth it. You see, he still hadn't told me you'd turned him down. So I agreed. And you kept silent.'

He got up and paced moodily round the room, to swing round and face her. 'How I must have hurt you!'

She sighed. 'From your viewpoint you were justified. It's the way it happened, but it's over. I just want to forget it.'

'I can't do that.'

'It's the only thing to do. I'm thankful you know, but . . .' Shakily she reached for her bag and sought her cigarettes. He stopped her and offered his own case.

'You know why I was so bitter?'

She looked at him over the small flame. 'It's natural. You love your brother. It left him crippled. Anyone would be bitter.'

'You're very understanding. But that isn't the entire reason.' He lit his own cigarette and weighed the lighter in his hand before dropping it into his pocket. 'I couldn't face the disillusion. You.'

'Me?'

His face was averted. 'I didn't want to believe all those things that the picture added up to. That you could be faithless to two men that I knew of—one of them my own brother—and were even prepared to amuse yourself with me. And the most disillusioning thing of all was *this*!'

He groped in the inside of his jacket and produced an envelope. Avoiding her gaze now, he dropped the blank manilla square on the soft lime damask by her side. 'You'd better check them and see if they're all here.'

She looked at the envelope, beginning to tremble and knowing what she would find. Her heart felt as though splinters of ice had pierced it and she could not move to obey his brusque command.

'Check them,' he repeated forcibly. 'Or must I do it for you?'

Numb with distress, she took out the contents and counted twelve prints and twelve negatives. Her eyes blurred and her hands were so clumsy that some of the photographs she hated so much slipped to the carpet and lay like mute testimony of accusation round her feet. Her mouth twisted and she turned away, striving not to break down.

'Oh, for heaven's sake!' Jordan towered over her. 'You don't need to be ashamed of—of what you see here. They're—you're so damned beautiful I want to—— Oh, for the love of heaven—if they're all there let's have them and——' He gathered the shadowy black squares together, his movements fierce and rough, and thrust them back into the envelope. 'Come on, I'll get you to the airport.'

Suddenly she broke free of her frozen trance and started up. 'No! Give them to me! They've brought me enough heartbreak. You're not going to have them and—and—— I'm going to destroy them!' she cried.

'No. *I* am going to destroy them!' he said savagely. '*I* am going to make sure no man ever gloats—that's what you were going to say, wasn't it? I'm going to make sure *that* never happens. Youth and innocence!' His face set in white lines of anger, he ripped the envelope

183

across and crushed the thickness in his hands. 'Now you can burn them!' He flung them in the hearth and with a visible effort regained his taut calm. He said huskily: 'Now, if you're ready . . .'

She stared at his angry eyes and felt limp. 'You—you sound almost as though you cared,' she whispered.

'Care! Yes, I care!' he raged. 'I've cared for three long years. And they've been hell on earth.'

The violence in him filled the room. She stood by the little pile of luggage and could not finish the mechanical move to begin gathering it up. She felt his presence at her shoulder.

'Yes, I've loved you. All the time. I stood back because my brother loved you—or thought he did. Then I found you were going to marry another man, before I even realised it was all over between you and Stuart. Now you know why I was so bitter, and why I had to see you before you left. I don't suppose it'll be much consolation for the hurt you must have suffered, but for what it's worth I've suffered as well.

'Now . . .' He moved away and the emptiness was there instantly where he had stood. 'I'll drive you to the airport.'

The echoes of his voice seemed to clamour in the silence after he stopped speaking. For a moment the room swam giddily, then every sense seemed to come into focus, and there was only his face that was clear and real.

'No! No——' she put out her hands, 'say that again! Did I dream it? Did you——?'

'You're not convinced of my sincerity? That I hate myself as much as you must hate me?' The force of his anger was spent and his voice had gone thin. 'What else can I say?'

Her mouth worked tremulously and she shook her

head. 'No, say what you said before. About caring. Because I—I can't believe you said you—you *loved* as well as—as cared.'

For a long moment he simply looked at her and at last she saw the agony in his eyes. She cried out and stumbled blindly towards him, and he opened his arms.

'Jordan ... Jordan!' she said against him, and clung to him with all the strength and longing in her body. 'Oh, Jordan,' she said again, and raised her head.

'Yes,' he said, and looked down at her before he crushed her mouth to his own.

She had no sense of time, how long they clung together, while the surge of aching hungry passion drove out everything but their need of each other. She did not remember stirring convulsively, her strength lost in his, so that he perceived her unsteadiness and said, 'I'm a bit light-headed too ...' drawing her none too steadily himself down to the settee. He took her face between his hands. 'Do you believe me now?'

The two things she wanted to believe were so fused in her being that she could only whisper, 'Yes,' and try to begin halting explanations even as his lips and his caresses were rendering words less necessary with every passing moment. At last she leaned breathlessly against him. 'Jordan ... no, please, I have to tell you ... It was always the same for me. That's why I couldn't marry Stuart. Because I'd fallen in love with you. That day on the beach ... that was when I knew, and——'

His mouth ceased its exploring. 'Yet you married another man.'

'I know.' She curled her fingers under his chin. 'I—I thought you despised me. I never even dreamed that you felt that way about me. If I'd been a little older and a little wiser ... I don't know.'

He was silent, and presently she said: 'Those photographs ... I had to go through with that, even though I never realised exactly what I was letting myself in for. Again, if I'd been a little bit older and wiser ... I never seemed to be able to see ahead like other girls I knew. But my mother was seriously ill, it was the only way I could raise the rest of the money we needed to send her abroad. So I—I had to do the modelling. Afterwards, when he sent me a set of them, I didn't know how I'd ever had the courage to go through with it. If he hadn't been so impersonal a man I doubt if I would. All he thought about was the light,' she added shakily.

Jordan's arms tightened in response to the small sigh that ran through her. He said against her hair, 'How much did he pay you?'

'Fifty pounds—it just turned the balance for us.'

'Fifty pounds? Good God! Is that all?'

'It seemed like a fortune then.' Something in his tone made her begin to wonder about something else. She looked up at him. 'Did—did you buy those for that calendar, and—and then change your mind?'

'What do you think?' His mouth had gone grave and tender.

She looked down, and for a moment his dark brows shadowed his eyes. He would never tell her of the extortionate sum a hard-headed commercially minded photographer had demanded for the best work he had ever done in his career, nor that for once he had lost his own arrogant granite-hard business acumen and all desire to bargain. He said thickly: 'Don't ever dare do such a thing again, do you hear?'

That he cared so much moved her to poignant response. There was still a strange haze of unreality clouding the joyous centre of enchantment in which she was bound with him, and still that sense of wondering if it was all real, that he knew the truth after the years of despair, and that he loved her. She said uncertainly, 'You do believe me...?'

'Of course I believe you,' he said quietly.

'And—and you understand about Blaise and me...?'

'Yes, I think so.' Suddenly he drew away and regarded her with intent eyes. 'But this time ... Gerda, I'm beginning to delve into that unselfish, compassionate heart of yours. I haven't the quiet, sagacious understanding of a Howard Durrel, nor am I a particularly unselfish type. In fact I'm proud and arrogant and demanding, and I hit back when I'm hurt. I'm rarely ill—but when I am you have to call out the entire medical brigade to deal with my aching little finger——' he interjected with a faint flush of humour, 'and I have little patience with fools. I know my faults, and I'm no saint. But I love you more than I've ever loved anyone or anything in this world. Is that enough?'

'If you can believe that I loved you all the time I thought you despised and hated me, and that I was going away because I couldn't bear the thought of being within reach of you and without you,' she said slowly, 'it may give you your answer. If it doesn't ... I can only go on loving you until you do believe me.'

'Will you marry me?'

'Yes, I'll marry you. Or,' she returned his gaze steadily, 'I'll live with you—because after this I can't live without you.'

The depth of emotion in his eyes and the wordless movement of his mouth conveyed his feelings more poignantly than any words, and with a small incoherent murmur she went back into his arms. A long while later he said unsteadily: 'How can you forgive me and love me like this when I look back and wonder how I can forgive myself?'

'No ...' she cradled his head, searched all the beloved planes of his face with a tender mouth, 'just don't ever let me go.'

'Never,' he said huskily. 'I love you and want you and need you too much, my darling. It'll take me a lifetime to make it all up to you. You know,' his voice deepened, and for a moment his caressing hands stayed their ardour, 'this has frightened me. It's taken my belief in myself, in my judgement, and in my attitudes to others. I was always so sure of myself, yet, all along, my heart wanted to believe in you, against everything my calculating brain argued.'

'Hush,' she put her finger to his lips, 'I can't bear to hear you condemn yourself. It's past now.'

'No,' his mouth shaped a kiss against her tender touch, 'I can't forget what it might have meant, what I'd have lost, if Rachel hadn't decided to tell me. I was wrong about her too,' he said despairingly. 'She suffered dreadfully all these years, knowing she was responsible for Stuart's accident and not being able to tell anyone. If I hadn't been so damned sure of myself I might have stopped to wonder why she was so fanatical in her devotion to him. I thought she was just another crazy kid, getting a sick kick out of flirting with a crippled boy. But it was the only way she could expiate her guilt. The only way she knew of to atone for what she had done.'

For once, and perhaps the only time she would ever experience it, Gerda felt stronger and wiser than this man who was so intensely strong in his beliefs and his own code. She did the only thing she could do at that moment of Jordan's bitter reappraisal of his heart and put her arms tightly round him.

'Rachel has been the wisest of us all,' she said softly, 'and now we must do as she has done. Stop looking back and start making our future, with faith in what we will make of it. No more vain regrets?' she whispered.

'No more vain regrets—ever,' he echoed.

But she knew the shadow of Stuart still lay on him, despite the awakening joy of their love, and she knew that this was the one shadow even her love could not erase for him, until ... She touched his face gently and put her hands, as with her heart, into his keeping. 'Has Stuart decided to have that operation?' she asked.

'Yes, at long last—probably within the next two weeks—as soon as we can make the arrangements.' Jordan paused, then added softly: 'I wondered ... if we could be married very soon. I know an enchanted place in the woods above the Rhine. We could have our honeymoon there, and it's near enough to visit Stuart and Rachel—she's staying with him, of course—and we could go and visit your mother—because I don't think you're going to make that plane today and I'm going to have to tear myself away from you and make a Continental call, and——' He looked down at her. 'Am I rushing you ahead too much?'

'No.' Though she smiled there was the glisten of moistness in her eyes. 'I want to be rushed, and I want to see Stuart walk again.'

* * *

Some six weeks later all her wishes had come true.

On a moonlit terrace by the Rhine, under the shadows of an old Gothic-spired castle straight out of fairy-tale enchantment, she watched the moon hang like a great pale silver orb above the pines, and her heart was filled with content. That morning they had watched Stuart stand and take his first steps for three years.

They had been unsteady, tentative, and they had been aided by loving hands, but they were steps, and they had taken him into the arms of a radiant girl whose mingled tears and laughter had brought a lump into Gerda's throat. And all Rachel had said was simply: 'There. I told you you could.'

'Faith and love,' said Jordan quietly, echoing her own thoughts with that unerring rapport that had developed so quickly between them in the two short weeks since their marriage.

The moon made silver of his hair as he stood at her side and closed his hand over hers where it rested on the old grey stone. He said, 'Now we can rejoice in our own happiness.'

She nodded, and they were silent again, until he said softly: 'Tell me again.'

'Tell you what?' With joy in her heart, she pretended puzzlement.

'Tell me you love me.'

'I love you, more than anything else in the world.'

He drew her into the curve of his arm, into content and joy and their own wonderful realm, and presently he said on a sigh: 'If only I could think of a thousand new ways to say it, a thousand new ways to show it.' He buried his mouth in her hair. 'You know, darling, that I'd give you the world if it were possible.'

She turned to him, full into his embrace, and shook her head. 'I don't want the world. I have you.'

Let Your Imagination Fly Sweepstakes

Rules and Regulations:

NO PURCHASE NECESSARY

1. Enter the Let Your Imagination Fly Sweepstakes 1, 2 or 3 as often as you wish. Mail each entry form separately bearing sufficient postage. Specify the sweepstake you wish to enter on the outside of the envelope. Mail a completed entry form or, your name, address, and telephone number printed on a plain 3″ x 5″ piece of paper to:

HARLEQUIN LET YOUR IMAGINATION FLY SWEEPSTAKES,
P.O. BOX 1280, MEDFORD, N.Y. 11763 U.S.A.

2. Each completed entry form must be accompanied by I Let Your Imagination Fly proof-of-purchase seal from the back inside cover of specially marked Let Your Imagination Fly Harlequin books (or the words "Let Your Imagination Fly" printed on a plain 3″ x 5″ piece of paper. Specify by number the Sweepstakes you are entering on the outside of the envelope.

3. The prize structure for each sweepstake is as follows:

Sweepstake 1 - North America

Grand Prize winner's choice: a one-week trip for two to either Bermuda; Montreal, Canada; or San Francisco. 3 Grand Prizes will be awarded (min. approx. retail value $1,375. U.S. based on Chicago departure) and 4,000 First Prizes: scarves by nik nik, worth $14. U.S. each. All prizes will be awarded.

Sweepstake 2 - Caribbean

Grand Prize winner's choice: a one-week trip for two to either Nassau, Bahamas; San Juan, Puerto Rico; or St. Thomas, Virgin Islands. 3 Grand Prizes will be awarded (Min. approx. retail value $1,650. U.S. based on Chicago departure) and 4,000 First Prizes: simulated diamond pendants by Kenneth Jay Lane, worth $15. U.S. each. All prizes will be awarded.

Sweepstake 3 - Europe

Grand Prize winner's choice: a one-week trip for two to either London, England; Frankfurt, Germany; Paris, France; or Rome, Italy. 3 Grand Prizes will be awarded. (Min. approx. retail value $2,800. U.S. based on Chicago departure) and 4,000 First Prizes: 1/2 oz. bottles of perfume, BLAZER by Anne Klein (Retail value over $30. U.S.). All prizes will be awarded.

Grand trip prizes will include coach round-trip airfare for two persons from the nearest commercial airport serviced by Delta Air Lines to the city as designated in the prize, double occupancy accommodation at a first-class or medium hotel, depending on vacation, and $500. U.S. spending money. Departure taxes, visas, passports, ground transportation to and from airports will be the responsibility of the winners.

4. To be eligible, Sweepstakes entries must be received as follows:
Sweepstake 1 Entries received by February 28, 1981
Sweepstake 2 Entries received by April 30, 1981
Sweepstake 3 Entries received by June 30, 1981
Make sure you enter each Sweepstake separately since entries will not be carried forward from one Sweepstake to the next.

The odds of winning will be determined by the number of entries received in each of the three sweepstakes. Canadian residents, in order to win any prize, will be required to first correctly answer a time-limited skill-testing question, to be posed by telephone, at a mutually convenient time.

5. Random selections to determine Sweepstake 1, 2 or 3 winners will be conducted by Lee Krost Associates, an independent judging organization whose decisions are final. Only one prize per family, per sweepstake. Prizes are non-transferable and non-refundable and no substitutions will be allowed. Winners will be responsible for any applicable federal, state and local taxes. Trips must be taken during normal tour periods before June 30, 1982. Reservations will be on a space-available basis. Airline tickets are non-transferable, non-refundable and non-redeemable for cash.

6. The Let Your Imagination Fly Sweepstakes is open to all residents of the United States of America and Canada, (excluding the Province of Quebec) except employees and their immediate families of Harlequin Enterprises Ltd., its advertising agencies, Marketing & Promotion Group Canada Ltd. and Lee Krost Associates, Inc., the independent judging company. Winners may be required to furnish proof of eligibility. Void wherever prohibited or restricted by law. All federal, state, provincial and local laws apply.

7. For a list of trip winners, send a stamped, self-addressed envelope to:
Harlequin Trip Winners List, P.O. Box 1401, MEDFORD, N.Y. 11763 U.S.A.
Winners lists will be available after the last sweepstake has been conducted and winners determined.
NO PURCHASE NECESSARY.

Let Your Imagination Fly Sweepstakes

OFFICIAL ENTRY FORM

Please enter me in Sweepstake No. _____

Please print:
Name _____

Address _____

Apt. No. _____   City _____

State/Prov. _____   Zip/Postal Code _____

Telephone No. area code
(   )

MAIL TO:
HARLEQUIN LET YOUR
IMAGINATION FLY SWEEPSTAKE No.
P.O. BOX 1280,
MEDFORD, N.Y. 11763 U.S.A.
(Please specify by number, the Sweepstake you are entering.)